Becca's e ~~~~~~~~~~ **ous**
cowboy ~~~~~~~~~~ **he**
doing he ~~~~~~~~~~

His mouth curled in a slow, satisfied smile.

"Marc, you run along and take your shower," she instructed.

Her son, who was fairly well behaved for a second-grade boy, picked that moment to exhibit his rare rebellious streak. "Hi, I'm Marc."

The cowboy smiled as he came closer, his long-legged stride graceful and annoyingly mesmerizing to watch. "I'm Sawyer."

"Mr. Sawyer, do you like pizza?" Marc said.

"As a matter of fact, I do." Sawyer grinned.

"Then you should—"

"Marc! Scoot." Becca tried to cut him off.

"—have dinner with us," her son invited.

Becca bit back a groan; Sawyer's eyes glittered with knowing humor as he met her gaze. He was amused by her discomfort, which did nothing to raise her opinion of him, but he had the decency to wait until her son was inside to laugh outright.

"Well," he said as the front door slammed, "at least one of you likes me."

Dear Reader,

Welcome back to Cupid's Bow! Or if this is your first visit to my fictional town, I'm so glad you're here.

The fun thing about returning to the same community over and over again is that the characters start to feel like family. I care about them and want them to be happy. When single mom Becca Johnston showed up in my first Cupid's Bow book, *Falling for the Sheriff*, she was a strong-minded woman who knew how to get stuff done, practically running the town through all of her volunteer efforts and her work on the town council. Becca has really grown on me over time, and I wanted to make sure this take-charge heroine met a hero worthy of her.

Enter rodeo cowboy Sawyer McCall, who needs a place to stay for a couple weeks and rents Becca's attic apartment. In many ways, he's Becca's opposite, guaranteed to drive her crazy. But sometimes the person you didn't know you wanted in your life is exactly who you need.

I hope you enjoy Becca and Sawyer's story and that you'll come back to Cupid's Bow! I'm already working on the next two books in the series. Follow me on Twitter, @TanyaMichaels, or like me on Facebook (AuthorTanyaMichaels) for updates about the series, anecdotes about my family and the writing life and to chat about favorite books and TV shows.

Hope to talk to you soon!

Tanya

THE COWBOY UPSTAIRS

—

Tanya Michaels

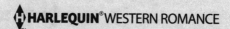

HARLEQUIN® WESTERN ROMANCE

Recycling programs
for this product may
not exist in your area.

ISBN-13: 978-0-373-75757-2

The Cowboy Upstairs

Copyright © 2017 by by Tanya Michna

Printed in U.S.A.

™ www.Harlequin.com

Tanya Michaels, a *New York Times* bestselling author and five-time RITA® Award nominee, has been writing love stories since middle-school algebra class (which probably explains her math grades). Her books, praised for their poignancy and humor, have received awards from readers and reviewers alike. Tanya is an active member of Romance Writers of America and a frequent public speaker. She lives outside Atlanta with her very supportive husband, two highly imaginative kids and a bichon frise who thinks she's the center of the universe.

Books by Tanya Michaels

Harlequin Western Romance

Cupid's Bow, Texas

Falling for the Sheriff
Falling for the Rancher
The Christmas Triplets

Harlequin American Romance

Hill Country Heroes

Claimed by a Cowboy
Tamed by a Texan
Rescued by a Ranger

The Colorado Cades

Her Secret, His Baby
Second Chance Christmas
Her Cowboy Hero

Texas Rodeo Barons

The Texan's Christmas

Visit the Author Profile page
at Harlequin.com for more titles.

For H. I love you.

Chapter One

"Sorry—I was trying to listen, but I got distracted by the hot cowboy in tight jeans." Even as Hadley made the apology, her gaze remained fixed across the dining room of the barbecue restaurant. The two women on either side of her craned their heads to look.

Across the table from the oglers, Becca Johnston sighed in exasperation. "Ladies, this is Cupid's Bow. Good-looking cowboys in Wranglers are a common occurrence. What's uncommon is a female mayor. So, could we focus?" If Becca won the election—no, *when* she won—she would be only the third woman in the town's hundred-year history to be mayor.

Sierra Bailey, seated next to Becca, smiled in encouragement, not at all distracted by the prospect of a hot cowboy—probably because she went home to her own cowboy every night. Locals had been placing bets on when her devoted rancher would officially pop the question. "You're going to make a wonderful mayor."

"Thank you." Becca truly appreciated the other woman's support and all the hours she'd spent volunteering on the campaign, in addition to her full-time job as a physical therapist. "You're forgiven for your poster idea." Sierra had suggested the slogan Vote for Our Favorite Control Freak!

"If it helps," Sierra said, "I meant it as a compliment. As Jarrett will tell you, I tend toward the bossy side myself."

In Becca's opinion, there was nothing freakish about wanting a life that was calm and controlled. Growing up in a house with six kids, she'd craved order. Now she planned to give that gift to her friends and neighbors.

Hadley refocused on the conversation, a glint in her dark eyes; the town librarian wasn't as blatantly outspoken as Sierra or Becca, but God help you if you defaced a book or interrupted patrons trying to read and study in peace. "In men, they call it leadership skills, but women get called 'bossy.' I say good for you—both of you—for not being afraid to take charge."

It isn't like anyone ever gave me a choice. Unwanted responsibility had been thrust on Becca as a kid. And again two years ago when her real estate agent husband fled town after a shady investment, leaving her a suddenly single mom struggling to pay the bills. Some money from a late uncle had helped her survive while she brainstormed new revenue streams, but survival wasn't enough. She wanted to triumph.

While Hadley had, thankfully, regained her concentration, Irene and Anita were still staring after the unseen cowboy.

"Who do you think he is?" Anita asked with a sigh. "Besides my future husband."

"Wait—none of you recognize him?" Becca swiveled in her chair, craning her head for a better look. She needed to know as many constituents as possible; if he was new to town, she should introduce herself. Then again, if a "hot cowboy" had just moved to Cupid's Bow, wouldn't she have heard the gossip by now? The local grapevine prided itself on speed and thoroughness.

She blinked at her first glimpse of the man. *Wow.* Hadley hadn't exaggerated his appeal. Unlike her friends, Becca wasn't usually drawn to rugged men. Her ideal type was more polished and urbane, like her ex-husband.

The man in the weathered straw cowboy hat stood facing local rancher Brody Davenport as they waited for a table; she could see only the stranger's profile, but it was impressive. Beneath the brim of his hat, a few curls of rich brown hair fell toward his eyes. His striking cheekbones were flawless and not even the unshaven stubble of an auburn-tinged beard lessened the effect of his strong jaw. And then there were his wide shoulders, corded forearms and, as promised, the breathtaking way he filled out his je—

Oh, *hell.* Suddenly Becca found her gaze locked with a pair of amused eyes. She couldn't tell their color from here, but the cocky merriment as he caught her staring was unmistakable. Heat flooded her cheeks, and she whipped her head back around. But the movement made her feel cowardly. Looking in his direction wasn't a crime, and she wasn't one to be intimidated by a man. Ignoring the prickle of embarrassment, she glanced back toward him and offered a casual, unimpressed smile.

He smirked.

Arrogant cowboy. She didn't want *him*; she'd just wanted his vote.

DESPITE BEING HUNGRY and eager to try the barbecue Brody claimed was the best in Texas, Sawyer McCall was irrationally annoyed when the hostess showed them to a booth around the corner. Following her meant he couldn't get a better look at the group of women on the other side of the restaurant—specifically, the woman with pale red-gold hair who'd been scoping him out with such frank appreciation before she'd studiously tried to pretend otherwise.

Too late, sweetheart. She couldn't erase the spark of awareness they'd shared.

Once seated at the booth, he and Brody ordered a couple sweet teas. While Sawyer studied the laminated menu, his friend began once again praising the restaurant.

"Back when I was doing the rodeo circuit, The Smoky Pig is what I missed most about Cupid's Bow." Brody smiled, looking happier than Sawyer had ever seen him. "Of course, that was before Jazz came back to town, or she would have been what I missed most." Last month, Brody had married a former high school classmate, Jasmine Tucker, who'd left Texas after graduation and returned to her hometown only a couple years ago. Brody had fallen hard.

Sawyer still couldn't believe the bronc rider he used to go out drinking with was someone's husband now. "I can't wait to meet her." He grinned slyly. "Especially if she's as gorgeous as you say she is." According to her proud new husband, Jasmine had been a model in New York City.

"No flirting with my wife, McCall." Brody shot him a mock glare before his tone returned to normal. "You know the only reason you weren't invited to the wedding is because it was so small and so far away, right?" Brody had admitted that he'd suggested the Caribbean ceremony because he'd wanted to prove he could be worldly, too—that marrying him didn't mean being "stuck" in Cupid's Bow.

"You sure the real reason you didn't invite me was because you were afraid she'd take one look at me and decide *I* was the better-looking cowboy?" Sawyer smirked, but then said, "Nah, I understand. I think it's great you two put a couple stamps in your passports. I've always had wanderlust myself." Granted, most of Sawyer's travels had been regional—Texas, New Mexico, Colorado, Wyoming.

"On-the-Move McCall. When was the last time you were home?"

Sawyer shrugged, as if the answer didn't matter. "My life's a thrilling blur of cattle drives and training horses, pretty cowgirls and small-town motels."

At the mention of motels, Brody frowned. "Are you sure you don't want to stay with us until after the trail ride? You'd be more than welcome."

Cupid's Bow was about to have its centennial celebration, a week of Western-themed festivities culminating in a three-day trail ride that would recreate the journey of the town's founders; on the strength of Brody's recommendation, Sawyer had been hired as one of the ride leaders. Getting here a week early allowed him plenty of time to catch up with his friend, a chance to compete in a rodeo in the next county and the opportunity to finish a series of articles he'd been writing for a Texas travel magazine. *Plus, you had nowhere else to be.* He hadn't been back to the family spread since his older brother had made it clear Sawyer was no more than a glorified ranch hand.

"I appreciate the offer of letting me bunk with you." Originally, that had been Sawyer's plan...or as close as he came to "planning" in advance. But he'd realized today just how smitten Brody was and how awkward the role of third wheel would be. "You and Jazz are newlyweds, though. You don't need me underfoot. I'll check into a hotel after lunch." It would be an added expense, but he'd had a good year between prize money and breeding rights for the bull he'd invested in. His only splurge was a new truck.

"Sure, there are a couple of hotels close by. Or you could—never mind."

Sawyer raised an eyebrow, his curiosity piqued. "What?"

"Well, Becca Johnston has a room to rent. Since you'll be staying for a couple of weeks, that might be more comfortable than a hotel, but she's—"

"You boys decided what you want to eat?" A blonde waitress with a polka-dot manicure and thick drawl set their drinks in front of them. "Sorry I took so long. Lunch rush."

Both men ordered their entrées, but as the waitress turned to go, Brody stopped her with a question. "Hey, Leanne, how would you describe Becca Johnston?"

"Terrifyingly efficient," she said over her shoulder.

"That pretty much nails it," Brody agreed. As the waitress walked away, he told Sawyer, "If you rented a room from Becca, your lodgings would be spotless, the meals would be tasty and she could answer any question you ever had about Cupid's Bow. But you don't want to cross her. Last man who did that is still missing."

Sawyer froze with his glass halfway to his mouth, sweet tea sloshing, but then decided his friend was messing with him. "You made up that last part."

"Exaggerated, maybe. But it's true no one knows where her ex-husband is—including Becca. Long story short, she's still pretty ticked. And she would hate you."

"What's wrong with me?" Sawyer demanded. "I've been told I have a winning personality."

"Becca likes structure and setting rules. While you...are a pain in the ass."

"But a charming one."

Brody snorted. "Not as charming as you think. Is that our food?" He perked up at the sight of Leanne carrying a tray in their direction.

"Do you have her phone number or address?"

"Leanne's?" Brody asked, sounding perplexed.

"Becca's."

"I'm telling you, it's a bad idea. Although, I suppose that's why you're pursuing it."

"What's that supposed to mean?"

Brody gave him a knowing glance. "Never met anyone who hates being told what to do more than you."

"It's not like I'm being stubborn for the sheer hell of it," Sawyer defended himself. "A private room is bound to offer more peace and quiet than a hotel filled with tourists in town for the centennial celebration."

"I'll give you directions to Becca's place, but it's your funeral if you track in mud or pick an argument with her."

"Pretty sure I can handle myself."

"Maybe. If not...can I have your truck?"

Chapter Two

Marc Johnston watched the soccer ball, a whirl of white and black as it came at him, and wished it would roll far away. Off the field. Into the street. His mama would never let him chase it into the street. No ball, no soccer practice. He could go home to play in his room! It was too hot outside.

But that was a dumb wish. If the ball rolled into the street, his mama would chase it down and bring it back to him. She'd told him a zillion times, "I'm always here for you." Not like his daddy, who'd gone away. Mama was never far.

Right now, she was coaching from the side of the field. "Kick the ball, Marc! You can do it!"

He swung his leg. It wasn't really a kick, not a good one. He brushed the side of the ball, which kept moving, and lost his balance as it rolled under his foot. He wobbled, then fell on his back, the sting just enough to make him suck in a breath. *Ow.*

Mama jogged toward him, her face crinkly with worry. She helped him up, brushing grass and dirt off his uniform. "You okay, champ?"

"I guess."

She patted him on the shoulder. "Maybe you should take a break and drink some water."

He'd rather have soda from the machine by the bleachers, but knew better than to ask. Mama handed him a water bottle, then turned to give instructions to Jodie Prescott, who was taller than Marc even though his birthday was before hers. He didn't like Jodie—she called him Shorty—but he was glad she was keeping Mama busy so he could go sit in the shade. There was another boy there, not in Marc's grade, playing on a Nintendo 3DS.

"Are you here for soccer practice?" Marc asked.

The kid grunted. "Does it look like I'm playing soccer? My dad's coaching my sister's team over there." He flung an arm toward another field without looking up from the screen. "I'm waiting."

"You're lucky you have a DS." *And lucky you have a dad.* And, also, lucky he didn't have to play soccer. "Can I have a turn?"

"No. But you can watch me." He scooted a little closer so that Marc could see the screen.

It was the best soccer practice ever. Marc almost forgot how hot it was. He even almost forgot about his mama, who had to call his name twice when it was time to go home. On their way to the van, the way she watched him made him feel bad for not trying harder at soccer.

She brushed the back of his shirt again. "We'd better get this straight in the washer if I'm going to get the stain out."

"Sorry." His mother didn't like stains. Or running in the house. Or when he forgot to swallow his food before telling her interesting stories, like how Kenny

Whittmeyer's pet snake got out of its cage. Marc had learned at dinner last night she also didn't like stories about Kenny Whittmeyer's pet snake.

"You don't have to apologize. You didn't do anything wrong—everyone falls down."

"Even you?" It was hard to imagine Mama falling. She never messed up.

"On occasion." She hit the key button that made the doors unlock. He got in the backseat, wishing he was big enough to sit in the front. It felt lonely back here.

Although she started the engine, she didn't drive anywhere. She looked at him in the mirror. "Marc, are you enjoying soccer?"

If he told her the truth, would he still have to play? *Probably.* She was the coach. They couldn't just quit the team. "Soccer's okay."

"You know you can talk to me, right?"

"Yes, Mama."

She sighed. She made that sound a lot. Marc didn't remember her doing it so much when his dad lived with them, but those memories were blurry, like when he tried to see underwater at the community pool.

"Mama? A girl in my class has parents with a divorce."

"Parents who are divorced."

"She says she lives with her dad in the summer. Is it summer soon?"

"Next month, after the election."

"Will I live with Daddy then?"

"No, I'm afraid not, champ." Her eyes were shiny in the mirror, like she might cry, and Marc wished he hadn't asked. "But I'll do my best to make sure you and I have a great summer. Okay?"

"Okay." He looked out his window. "Is Mr. Zeke coming back?" For months, the bald, smiling man had been around their house, making what Mama called ren-o-vations. Mr. Zeke had shown Marc cool drills and saws.

"Not anytime soon. The attic's finished now, so he's moved on to his next job. But now that the attic apartment is ready to rent, maybe we'll have guests."

That would be nice. It would be even better if whoever came to stay with them was as cool as Mr. Zeke.

BECCA HAD MIXED feelings about her son's silence on the drive home. On the one hand, she'd had a very long day and appreciated the few minutes of peace. But she was worried; quiet reflection was not the seven-year-old's natural state. Was he still in pain from his fall? *More likely he's still in pain from his father's defection.* The questions about when he would see his dad, followed by whether or not the general contractor would be back, made it pretty clear that he missed having a man to look up to in his life.

Her throat burned. Nothing mattered more to her than her son, but she couldn't be everything to him. The town's upcoming centennial celebration was taking up her time for the next couple weeks. But maybe after that, she could invite Zeke, a widower in his late fifties, over for dinner—a home-cooked thank-you for a job well done.

By the time they rolled into the driveway, the stillness in the minivan was becoming oppressive. This called for emergency measures. "How about I order pizza for dinner while you take your shower?"

The excited whoop from the backseat made her

smile. She'd barely pulled the keys from the ignition before her son flew out of the vehicle and up the three wide porch steps. There, he sat dutifully to remove his cleats. She took a minute to stare at the house, gleaming white in the Texas sunshine, and remembered the day she and Colin had moved in. It was a beautiful two-story home, complete with a porch swing, surrounding rosebushes and gorgeous maple trees in the yard. It had all symbolized how far she'd come from an overcrowded double-wide trailer on a gravel lot. To her, this house had been the castle at the end of the fairy tale.

It still can be. She clenched her fists at her sides, summoning determination. Okay, yes, Colin had turned out to be more fraudulent frog than prince. But she didn't need him for a happy ending. She would become mayor and raise a wonderful son.

"Mama, I can't get this knot out."

Joining Marc at the top of the steps, she knelt down over his shoe. Her promise of pizza must have really improved his mood, because by the time she'd unlaced both cleats, he was happily chatting away. She didn't even register the sound of the vehicle at the bottom of the driveway until the door closed.

"Excuse me," a deep masculine voice called, "are you by any chance Becca J—"

As she turned, the man stopped dead, recognition striking them both. The cowboy from the bar? What was he doing here? Stalking her?

"You," he breathed. His mouth curled in a slow, satisfied smile. "You're the woman who was checking m—"

"Marc, you run along and take your shower," she instructed. She was about to throw this man off her property. It was probably better that her son didn't witness it…or overhear any of the man's lewd commentary on what she may have been "checking." Unbelievable. She'd ogled a stranger *once* since her divorce, and he'd followed her home. What were the odds?

"Uh, Mama? The door's locked."

Right. She knew that. She fiddled with the key, but the dead bolt got only part of her attention. The sense that she could feel the man's gaze on her was distracting. "There you go, champ." She swung the main door wide open, expecting her son to reach for the handle on the inner screen door.

Instead, he hesitated, waving at the approaching cowboy. "Hi, I'm Marc."

The cowboy smiled, his long-legged stride graceful and annoyingly mesmerizing to watch. "I'm Sawyer."

Marc's eyes widened as he caught sight of the man's gold belt buckle, etched with a cowboy on the back of a bucking horse; Becca read the word *champion* before realizing that she was staring in the direction of the man's groin, and averted her eyes. "Did you win a rodeo?" her son asked.

"Quite a few."

"That is so cool! Maybe I'll ride in a rodeo someday," Marc said, surprising Becca. He'd never expressed any interest in that. "I take riding lessons from Ms. Meredith. She's nice, but I like Ms. Kate better. She's my piano teacher. She gives me cookies."

Hearing him list his teachers out loud, Becca mentally kicked herself. She'd inadvertently surrounded him with women. Why hadn't she checked to see if Jarrett Ross was taking on any more riding students over at his ranch? In Becca's defense, Marc's soccer coach was supposed to have been a man. But when he'd broken his leg the first week of the season, she'd stepped up to fill the void.

Sawyer winked down at her son. "Keep at that piano practice. The ladies love musicians."

Yeah, that's what her seven-year-old needed— advice on picking up women. From the cocky way Sawyer carried himself, she just bet he had plenty of experience in that area. "Ladies also love hygiene," she said wryly. "Now about your shower…"

Marc opened the screen door. "Back in a minute!"

"Take your time and do the job right," Becca cautioned. "There's no rush."

"But I'm *hungry*. If I hurry, I get pizza faster. Mr. Sawyer, do you like pizza?"

"As a matter of fact, I love it."

"Then you should—"

"Marc! Scoot."

"—have dinner with us," her son invited.

Becca bit back a groan; Sawyer's eyes glittered with humor as he met her gaze. He was amused by her discomfort, which did nothing to raise her opinion of him.

"Well," he said as Marc disappeared inside, "at least one of you likes me."

Now that he was on the step just below her, she could see his eyes were green, flecked with gold, and she hated herself for noticing. "If you'll excuse me for a moment," she said tightly, "I need to call in an order for pizza." That would give her an opportunity to regain her composure.

He smirked. Didn't the man have any other expressions? "Want to know what toppings I like?"

She shot him a look that should have vaporized him

on the spot, leaving nothing but his memory and scorch marks on the sidewalk.

"I'll just wait here then," he said, moving past her to make himself comfortable on the porch swing. He even took his hat off and ran a hand through his brown hair. In the sunlight, a few threads shone a deep coppery red, much darker than her own strawberry blond.

His hair was thick, wavy, and she wondered errantly if it was soft to the touch. *Rebecca Ruth Baker Johnston, pull yourself together.* Just because she hadn't had sex in the two years since Colin skipped town was no reason to become unhinged in hormonal desperation. She marched into the house, locking the door behind her. No matter how good-looking he was, Sawyer was a stranger; she was a single woman with a child to protect. She called the pizza place, but she was so preoccupied that there was no telling what she ordered. For all she knew, instead of a large pepperoni pie with extra olives, dinner tonight might be a piece of garlic bread and six liters of soda.

Well, that's what she got for stalling. Her philosophy had always been to tackle problems efficiently, then put them behind her. Time to figure out why this cowboy was here and send him on his way. She returned to the porch, her tone brisk as she asked, "So is Sawyer your first name or last?"

"First. Sawyer McCall." He extended a hand. "Pleasure to meet you. Officially."

Her fingers brushed over his in something too brief to qualify as a handshake before she pulled away. "Becca Johnston. What are you doing here?" *Besides bonding with my son and trying to mooch free pizza.*

"Brody Davenport sent me. I don't know if you happened to notice while you were undressing me with your eyes—"

She exhaled in an outraged squeak.

"—but he's who I was having lunch with. Brody and I are old friends. He contacted me a few months ago about coming to town to help with the centennial trail ride and to finally meet Jasmine. I need a place to stay."

That place sure as hell wouldn't be under *her* roof. "There are two motels in the Cupid's Bow area," she said. "I can draw you maps to both of them."

He bobbed his head. "Yeah, Brody said you were pretty much an expert on this town—which would be useful to me, since I'm writing a travel piece. Brody also said that if I stayed here, the room would be spotlessly clean and the food would be excellent."

She bit the inside of her lip. When she'd had the bright idea to rent out her attic, she'd been thinking more in terms of single women who might feel vulnerable staying alone at a hotel, or who would appreciate bubble baths in the spacious claw-foot tub. Maybe she could even rent the room as a long-term apartment to a woman like herself, divorced and needing to regroup. She certainly hadn't considered giving the key to a smug, sexy stranger. "I think I would prefer female tenants," she said. "At least until I get a guard dog."

He raised an eyebrow. "You don't strike me as a dog person."

She wasn't; training and grooming seemed like a lot of work when she was already stretched thin with limited hours in the day. But she resented being pigeonholed. "You don't know anything about me, Mr. McCall."

"No, but from what Brody said…" He cleared his throat, looking sheepish.

Ah. So there'd been more to the rancher's characterization of her than the promise of a clean house and good food. All Sierra's teasing about being a control freak echoed in Becca's head.

"Do you currently have any female tenants scheduled?" Sawyer asked.

"Well, not yet."

"I can pay up front. Cash. And I can give you a list of references, including Brody and his aunt Marie, to assure you I'm not some whack-job."

She'd known Marie Davenport, a now-retired 911 operator, for years. And there was no denying Becca could use the money; her salary running the community center and her stipend as a town-council member were barely a full-time income. That's why she'd decided to invest in renovating her attic to an apartment in the first place, so she could rent it to a paying customer. *Yes, but…him?*

Becca had spent her life mastering the art of structure. During the happier moments of her marriage, she'd relaxed, grown complacent, and she'd paid for it with scandal and divorce. Now, she was more determined than ever to keep her life smooth and orderly. Sawyer McCall might be smooth, with his glib manner and roguish smile, but instinct screamed that life would be anything but orderly with this cowboy living upstairs.

"Mr. McCall, I really don't think—"

The screen door banged open and a mini tornado gusted across the porch in the form of her son, his green dinosaur pajamas plastered to the wet chest and limbs he hadn't bothered to dry. "You're still here! Are you staying for pizza? Mama, can I show him my space cowboys and robot horses?"

Becca studied her son's eager face and tried to recall the last time she'd seen him look so purely happy. "Mr. McCall and I aren't finished talking yet, champ. Why don't you go set the table for three?" She wasn't convinced she would rent the room to Sawyer, but a slice of pizza was a small price to pay for her son's beaming smile.

Marc disappeared back inside as quickly as he'd come.

She took a deep breath. "The attic apartment has its own back stair entrance and a private bathroom. No kitchen, although there's a small refrigerator up there for beverages and snacks. Whoever I rent the room to is welcome to join Marc and me for meals—but in exchange, I was hoping to find someone with a bit of child-care experience. Occasional babysitting in trade for my cooking." She'd only just now had that brainstorm, realizing how much it would mean to Marc to be around a man, but it sounded plausible. And if Sawyer said no, it would help justify turning him away.

He shrugged. "Sounds reasonable. I'm no child-care expert, but I've worked with kids at equestrian camps and on family trail rides."

She sighed, regretting what she was about to say before it even left her mouth. "Then, assuming your references check out, you've got a deal, Mr. McCall."

His grin, boldly triumphant and male, sent tiny shivers up her arms. "When do I get to see my room?"

Chapter Three

Sawyer braved his landlady's glare, her blue eyes like the center of a flame. Fiery was a good description for her—hot, but projecting the aura that a man should stay back for his own safety. At the restaurant earlier, he'd seen her sitting down. She was a lot taller than he'd expected, trim and shapely in her polo shirt and shorts. When he first drove up, her kid had been wearing a numbered practice jersey; Becca wore a whistle on the cord around her neck. Team coach, maybe? She seemed like the kind of person who wanted to be in charge.

And not at all like a woman who changed her mind easily. Despite his claims at lunch that he was charming and likable, Sawyer was almost surprised she'd agreed to rent him the room. Her expression when she'd first seen him in the driveway had suggested she was more likely to back over him than take him in as a guest.

"Come on," she said irritably. "We might have enough time before the pizza comes for you to see the room." She opened the door, but stood there, barring his entrance as she studied his boots. "You can leave those on the porch."

Her tone rankled. He wasn't her damn kid. "Yes, ma'am. I promise to wash my hands before eating, too."

She gave him another narrow-eyed glare. *Probably deserved that one.* Instead of halfheartedly apologizing for his sarcasm, he gave her a winning smile. She pressed a finger to her forehead as if physically pained.

Maybe he should stay at a hotel, after all. Brody was right about him—Sawyer had a habit of provoking bossy people. Wouldn't sharing a house with a woman who already disliked him needlessly complicate life?

Nah. In only a matter of minutes, he'd convinced her to change her mind about renting to him. In a matter of weeks, he could win her over entirely. Sawyer liked a challenge. Besides, in the unlikely event that he failed, it was just a few weeks out of his life. After that, he'd be putting Cupid's Bow behind him.

He placed the boots neatly by the front door. "After you."

Brody hadn't exaggerated when he predicted the place would be spotless. The hardwood floors gleamed; the creamy walls looked freshly painted. There were no toys scattered about or fingerprint smudges. If he hadn't seen Marc with his own eyes, Sawyer never would have believed a little boy lived here.

The narrow hallway opened up into a living room and Sawyer winced. "Is my room this...pink?" The low-backed sofa and two armchairs were all the same shade, coordinating with a striped circular rug that took up most of the floor.

"Mauve," she corrected, studying the furniture with him. "With cranberry accents."

Cranberry? An Aggies football fan, he would have called the dark throw pillows and decorative candles "maroon." At least then it would be showing team support for Texas A&M.

Her tone was defensive. "I think it looks nice, but to answer your question, no, this isn't the color scheme I used in the attic." She suddenly brightened. "Still, I completely understand if the accommodations here aren't to your liking. I can still give you directions to either of those hotels."

He should probably be insulted that she was so eager to get rid of him. "I'm sure the room will be just fine. Even if the bed's lumpy, with mismatched sheets, it'll be better than all the times I've slept on the ground during a trail ride or stayed in a crappy motel room." He'd been to rodeos in luxury Vegas settings and tourist-destination stockyards, but those weren't the norm.

"Mr. McCall, I do not make up beds with mismatched sheets."

He couldn't help grinning at her affronted tone; the woman took her linens seriously. "I've always cared more about what happens between the sheets than about whether they match."

She sucked in a breath, but the doorbell rang, saving him from a potentially blistering retort. Redirecting her anger, she glared toward the front of the house. "That better not be the pizza already!"

Was she that set on having events unfold according to her timeline? "Most people are happy when they don't have to wait long for delivery."

"There are three regular drivers," she said, as she dug through her purse. "But Keesha only works weekends. Which leaves D. B. Janak, who I happen to know has the flu, because I ran into his girlfriend at the store, and Callum Breelan, who is proving to be just as bad as his disreputable uncles." Money in hand, she strode toward the door, rattling off the rest of her explanation over her shoulder. "Only seventeen and he already has one speeding ticket and two warnings— Deputy Thomas went easy on him. I don't need lead-foot Callum using my dinner as an excuse to mow down pedestrians and small animals."

Sawyer blinked at the unexpected blast of information. She'd been talking too fast about people he'd never met for him to process all of it. The upshot seemed to be Becca knew *a lot* about her neighbors. And had strong opinions.

While she stood at the door haranguing the delivery boy about his driving habits, Sawyer found his way down the hall to a huge kitchen, the kind that was big enough to include a full-size dining room table and china cabinet. Marc stood on his tiptoes at a marble-topped island, trying to pour lemonade into a red plastic superhero cup. Sawyer lunged forward, taking the pitcher from the boy's hands just as it started to wobble.

"Here, better let me get that for you. I'm guessin' your mama doesn't like spills."

The boy shook his head, eyes wide. They were the same color as Becca's. "She hates messes. And snakes, even though they're cool."

"Not all of them," Sawyer said. He'd had a few close encounters with rattlesnakes and copperheads he'd rather not think about. He eyed the pitcher on the counter, noting the slices of fresh lemon bobbing inside it; obviously, Becca did not serve lemonade that came from powder. "Where can I find a glass?"

Marc directed him to a cabinet next to the stainless steel refrigerator—not that it was easy to see the silver steel beneath the clutter. The kitchen was pristine—no dirty dishes in the sink, no mail sitting on the counter—

but the fridge was practically wallpapered in Marc's schoolwork, crayon drawings and photos. As he looked closer, Sawyer realized there were also a number of newspaper clippings that all seemed to be about Cupid's Bow events. One mentioned a Watermelon Festival, while another—

"Can I help you find something in particular?" Becca asked from behind him, her voice icy.

Busted. He straightened, making light of his snooping. "Guess I was just curious about the family I'll be staying with, trying to reassure myself that you and Marc here aren't—" he'd been about to say ax murderers, but murder jokes weren't appropriate in front of the little boy "—aliens from outer space." That made the kid giggle, and Sawyer winked at him. "Or dangerous robots. Or spies for the CIA!"

"That's ridiculous," Becca said, exasperated. "Our CIA handler is the one who gave us all that fake documentation to support our covers in the first place."

Sawyer rocked back on his heels. So she did have a sense of humor? Good to know. The next few weeks were looking up already. He grinned at her, but she turned away to set the pizza on the table, almost as if she were hiding her smile.

"Marc was kind enough to show me where the glasses are," he said, pulling one from the cabinet. "The lemonade looks delicious. Want me to pour you some, too?"

She cocked her head, seeming confused by the question.

"Becca?"

"Sorry, I'm not used to someone else serving me in my own kitchen. Lemonade would be lovely, thank you."

Sawyer remembered Brody mentioning an ex-husband who'd bailed on her and the boy. How long had she been alone, that something as simple as someone else pouring her a drink was jarring?

"Wait, Marc, slow down!" Becca batted her son's hand away from the open box as Sawyer joined them at the table. "The pizza's still pretty hot."

"Guess what, Mama? I've decided not to get a pet snake when I grow up."

"Oh, good." She dropped her arm around his shoulders in a brief hug. "I was going to talk you out of it, anyway, but this saves me the trouble."

The oval table was big enough to seat eight. Marc and Becca sat next to each other, toward the center, and Sawyer went around to the other side, taking the chair opposite Marc.

"It's so cool Mr. Sawyer could have dinner with us!" Marc grinned so broadly that Sawyer noticed for the first time that the kid was missing one of his bottom teeth.

Becca hesitated. "Actually, he might be staying a few days. Or longer."

"In the new upstairs room?" Marc shot out of his seat with a whoop of excitement.

"Marc Paul Johnston, what kind of table manners are those?"

"Sorry." He slid back into his chair, his tone sheepish. But he was still smiling.

Sawyer locked his gaze on his plate, not wanting to make eye contact with the kid. If he returned Marc's grin, Becca might think he was encouraging the boy's rambunctious behavior. Besides, it was discomfiting to be the source of so much joy. He'd signed autographs for kids at rodeos and assisted tourists with children, but he'd never had prolonged exposure to one. *You'll be an uncle soon.* Would he be close to his future niece or nephew? Doubtful. He sure as hell wasn't close to his brother.

Charlie hadn't even been the one to share the news that he and his wife were expecting; Sawyer's mom had told him the last time he talked to her on the phone. The next day, Charlie had sent a terse email and Sawyer had replied with dutiful congratulations. That had been a couple weeks ago, and he could still hear his mother's chiding tone in his head.

"Gwen's due at the end of October. Surely you'll want to arrange your schedule so that you can be here?"

He'd told her he really couldn't say what his schedule would be in the fall, but that he'd be in touch. Then he'd quickly found an excuse to get off the phone. The truth was, even if he could make it, what would be the point? His sister-in-law was a nice lady, but her own family lived close to the ranch, so she had plenty of support. And as for Charlie… Ever since his older brother had returned to the ranch from college, the two of them could barely be in the same room without an argument erupting. Their father always sided with Charlie. Their mother just wanted everyone to get along. In her mind, that meant Sawyer—the outnumbered younger son—should cave.

"Something wrong with your pizza?" Becca asked tentatively.

Sawyer realized he was scowling. "Uh…you were right about it being hot. I burned the roof of my mouth," he lied.

"Kenny Whittmeyer's dad burned his hand when

he took Kenny and me camping," Marc volunteered. "We were roasting marshmallows and he said a whole *bunch* of bad words. I—"

A trumpet sound came from beneath the table, and Becca shifted in her seat, pulling a cell phone from the pocket of her shorts. She glanced at her son. "You know I'm only checking this because of the race, right?"

He nodded, informing Sawyer, "Mama has a no-phone rule at the table. But we make ex-sections 'cause of the race."

"Exceptions," Becca corrected absently, reading a text. She frowned, but put the phone away rather than responding. "Who wants the last slice of pizza?"

Sawyer shook his head, letting the growing boy snag it, and reached for his glass. "What's this race you mentioned? Are you a runner?" He could easily imagine her in a marathon. She seemed disciplined enough, and judging from her toned figure, she did something to keep in shape.

"Not literally. I'm running for mayor."

Sawyer choked on his lemonade.

"You find that funny, Mr. McCall?"

Hell, yes. Weren't politicians supposed to kiss babies and suck up to people? Becca was far too imperious for that. She hadn't even been able to pay for a pizza without lecturing the hapless delivery boy.

She misinterpreted the smile he was fighting. "I'll have you know that women are *every bit* as capable as—"

"Whoa. No argument here. I've known plenty of badass women."

"So what's the big joke?" She challenged, those eyes sparking again.

He doubted there was any answer that wouldn't get him in trouble. Might as well go with the truth. "The idea of you courting votes is a *little* funny, don't you think? You seem like someone who speaks her mind, whether the opinion is popular or not."

"And that's bad? Community leaders should be honest and straightforward."

"In theory, sure." Feeling Marc's gaze on him reminded Sawyer that there was a seven-year-old listening to his cynicism. "But don't listen to me. I'm just an outsider. What do I know about the people of Cupid's Bow?"

Becca stood, gathering up the empty plates. "About that—you being an outsider? Would you mind finishing your lemonade on the porch and enjoying the evening breeze while I call Brody Davenport? I need to start checking your references."

"No problem." He scraped his chair back. "Checking up on me is the responsible thing to do."

She gave him a smile that was part apology, part amusement. "Well, I'd hate to accidentally rent the room to a dangerous alien robot."

"That would be awesome!" Marc said.

"Which," she told him affectionately, "is why *I'm* the one who makes the decisions around here."

Sawyer understood not letting a second grader run the household, but alien robots aside, he was pretty sure Becca preferred to be the one making decisions no matter who was involved. *Just like Charlie.* But a hell of a lot prettier.

AFTER BECCA FINISHED her phone call, she tucked in Marc, who was supposed to read for thirty minutes, then go to sleep. From the excitement on his small freckled face, she suspected he wouldn't be falling asleep anytime soon. She wasn't sure yet how she felt about her new tenant, but she had to admit he'd been great with her son.

She should go thank him. And let him know the room was officially his.

She stepped onto the front porch, where the heat was sticky in comparison to the air-conditioned house but not intolerable. Intolerable came in August. Sawyer glanced up from the swing with that too-appealing grin that could've belonged to a movie star; the spectacularly vivid sunset behind him added a cinematic effect. The only thing missing was a musical score. Becca told herself she was unaffected and had always liked books more than films, anyway.

"Did Brody vouch for me?" he asked.

"He said I should kick you to the curb—that you're a pain in the ass who likes to get his own way."

Sawyer shrugged. "Well, who *doesn't* like to get his way?"

Hard to argue that. Brody had also said Sawyer was dependable, loyal and never drank to excess or let himself get goaded into bar fights, like a few of their former rodeo friends.

"Let me show you the room. Pay me cash for tonight, and you can decide in the morning how long you're staying, after you've had a chance to judge the accommodations for yourself." She almost said something about making sure the bed was comfortable, but stopped herself, recalling his comment about sheets earlier. She did not need to hear any jokes about what took place in his bed.

He unfolded himself from the swing, and she took a moment to appreciate the novelty of being with someone taller than she was. Only a handful of men here in Cupid's Bow were. In elementary school, she'd hated being the tallest in her class—probably the tallest in the whole school. But she'd decided her height was an advantage at home. Towering over her siblings helped her secure their obedience.

She'd foolishly taken it as a good sign that she and her ex-husband had been the same height; she'd joked to a friend that there was no better way to start a life together than seeing eye to eye. *Nice symbolism, lousy results.* Pushing aside memories of her failed marriage, she opened the door.

After Sawyer's reaction to her "pink" furniture, she was hyperaware of her feminine decorating touches as she led him to the back of the house. The hallway was lined with pictures of her and Marc in scallop-edged and filigree frames. A curved glass vase of yellow roses sat on the kitchen counter. The delicately patterned stair runner that went up to the second floor looked like lace from a distance.

Although Sawyer would never see it, her own bedroom was a frilly, silky haven complete with scented candles and ornamental pillows too small to have any practical purpose. Becca prided herself on being sensible and getting things done; she wielded coupons with genius, killed bugs and occasional rodents and could single-handedly fix a lot of the plumbing problems that came with home ownership. But after growing up in a grungy trailer with three brothers—and later, two sisters who wore their brothers' hand-medowns—she couldn't resist surrounding herself with soft, girlie indulgences.

The staircase felt uncharacteristically cramped with Sawyer on the steps behind her, as if he was closer than decency permitted. She suddenly wished she was wearing a loose T-shirt that hung down past her butt instead of a tucked-in polo shirt. *Don't be ridiculous. There's nothing wrong with your butt, and you don't care about his opinion of it, anyway.* Although...turnabout being fair play, it would make them even if he noticed her body. She'd certainly ogled his earlier today.

"The master bedroom, guest room and Marc's room are all on this floor," she said, as they reached the landing. "The attic is one more flight up."

The extra trip involved a narrow spiral staircase with an iron railing.

A quarter of the way up, Sawyer huffed out an exaggerated breath. "Good thing I'm in shape. But just in case, do you know CPR?"

Of course she did. She'd taken half a dozen first-aid and emergency preparedness classes when she'd been pregnant. But she said nothing, refusing to encourage any jokes about her mouth on Sawyer's—which didn't stop the forbidden image from flashing through her mind. The man might be cocky and unapologetically brash, but he'd demonstrated moments of thoughtfulness this evening, too. The right combination of confidence and attentiveness could make for a devastating kiss. Her toes curled inside her sneakers.

Get a grip, Rebecca.

She had no business thinking about kissing her tenant. Or anyone else, until the centennial celebration was over. She was the chairwoman of the centennial committee, and a flawless series of public events would help her win this election. *Stick to the plan.*

While she was at it, she needed to stick to an impersonal, informative tour—more letting him know where the clean towels were, less imagining where his hands would be if he were kissing her. "Coming up from the outside will be a lot easier than this. The house was built into a little bit of a hill, so the staircase is short. Not to mention, using the private entrance will be less disruptive to me and Marc if you keep late hours."

Would he be staying out late? He was a good-looking single man in a town with two bars and a popular dance hall. Opportunities abounded. Her stomach clenched. What if he wasn't alone when he came back to his room at night?

She bit the inside of her lip, conflicted. She didn't really have the right to insist he be celibate while he was in Cupid's Bow…but she *was* responsible for the impressionable child sleeping one floor below.

The attic door wasn't a standard size; they both needed to duck slightly to go through it. Inside the room, the ceiling was comprised of crazy, irregular angles, but nothing that Sawyer would bang his head on.

"Cozy," he said, looking around. "I meant that in a good way, promise."

To their left was a queen-size bed covered in a quilt she'd won in an auction at the Cupid's Bow Watermelon Festival; to the right was a small sitting area with two antique chairs, a bookshelf and a modest-sized, flat-screen TV. He would also have his own microwave and mini fridge. The windows were tiny, reminiscent of the portholes on a ship. When she'd had Zeke install the back door, she'd also asked him to include sidelights for a little more sunshine.

"See? No pink," she told him. The general decorating theme up here was "furniture I didn't need anywhere else in the house" but she'd tried to tie everything together with navy and cream. "Bathroom's around the corner. Everything you need should be in the linen closet, but let me know if I overlooked anything."

He poked his head through the doorway and laughed. "I haven't seen a tub like that since Granny's house."

"And where did Granny live? Brody talked about how long he'd known you, but didn't mention where you're from."

"Most of my family is west of here, toward the Hill Country. We have a… My father and brother run a spread in Kerr County."

"Are you close to them?"

He rocked back on his heels, thumbs in his belt loops. "Let's just say, I thought it would be better to strike out on my own."

"I can relate to that," she said softly, more to herself than him. Her earliest memories were of her trucker father kissing her goodbye and telling her to take care of "Mama and the baby" while he was gone. Her younger brother Everett hadn't even been a year old when their mother got pregnant with the twins. That had been a complicated pregnancy, with a lot of doctor-mandated bed rest, and Odette Baker had never really been the same afterward. By the time Becca was ten and the first of her sisters was born, she was actively fantasizing about the day she could move away.

"You're not from Cupid's Bow?" Sawyer asked. "With you running for mayor and talking like you know everybody in town, I figured you were born here."

"Nope. I grew up a little over an hour away." Cupid's Bow was separated from her hometown by eighty minutes...and a world of experience. Back home, all she'd ever wanted was to escape. From the minute Colin had brought her to Cupid's Bow, all she'd wanted was to belong. She *loved* it here. She loved the people and the open spaces. She loved that she could see an unending blue horizon unimpeded by skyscrapers, and brilliant stars not strangled by city lights or air pollution. "Cupid's Bow is the perfect size for me. The population's under four thousand, so it has small-town charm, but it's not so small that the only businesses are eponymous."

He raised an eyebrow. "E-pony-what-now?"

"Self-named. In the town I grew up in, there was one restaurant—Ed's Diner. Never mind that it sucked. And the only place to get your hair cut was Shirl's. Owned and operated by—"

"Let me guess—Shirl?"

She nodded. "There's healthy market competition here in Cupid's Bow, but we haven't been overrun by generic franchises. It's the perfect balance."

"And you want to become mayor so you can maintain that balance?"

"Well, that...and I like telling people what to do."

He laughed. "I feel sorry for the poor slob running against you."

"That would be the incumbent," she said, her mood darkening as she remembered Sierra's text from earlier. Last election, Mayor Lamar Truitt had run unopposed. Displeased that Becca had the nerve to challenge him, he was constantly looking for chances at passive-aggressive sabotage. "Which reminds me, I have some phone calls to make. I should let you settle in." She reached in her pocket for the key to the attic entrance, but hesitated. "I'll have breakfast on the table at 6:00 a.m. I know that's early, but I have to get Marc to school."

"Actually, I'll already be gone by then. Brody and I plan to get in some sunrise fishing before heading to look at livestock. He's thinking about expanding his herd."

She wasn't so much interested in his plans tomorrow as she was in making a necessary point. "While you're here, Mr. McCall—"

"Sawyer." He gave her a chiding smile. "I insist."

"While you're here, it's best if you come down to breakfast alone."

His smile faded to a perplexed expression. "I just told you, I won't be here for breakfast."

"I don't mean tomorrow, I mean in general. It would be better if you don't bring any…guests to breakfast."

Comprehension lit those gold-green eyes. After a moment, he smiled. "I see. Rest assured, I will only show up at the breakfast table as a party of one."

Relieved to have that settled, she wished him a good night and turned toward the door.

She was on the staircase when he called from behind her, "No need to bring guests down for food, anyway. I can just keep the fridge stocked and serve breakfast in bed."

Chapter Four

It was still dark outside when Brody called to say he was turning onto Becca's street, but, judging by the enthusiastic dawn chorus of birds outside Sawyer's room, sunrise was coming. He went down the flight of stairs behind the house and had just reached the bottom when a pair of headlights shone across the driveway. He swung open the passenger door of Brody's pickup, greeted by the welcome smell of coffee.

"You survived the night," Brody observed.

Sawyer climbed into the cab. "Sorry to disappoint you—I know you want my truck if Becca decides to spike my food with hemlock. Give her time. I don't generally drive people to homicidal rages until they've known me at least twelve hours. I hear you were completely unhelpful as a character reference, by the way."

"You wanted me to lie to her? Cupid's Bow is my home." Brody sipped from a travel mug, handing a second one to Sawyer. "After you get on her nerves and she runs you out of town—or buries you in the city park—*I* still have to face her."

"Don't want to run afoul of the new mayor, huh?"

"It'll be interesting to see who wins the election. Truitt's sort of...blandly competent. Not someone who inspires devotion, but his cronies have a fair amount of combined influence in town. Becca could be great, if anyone bothers to vote for her. She's outspoken—"

"Gee, I hadn't noticed."

"—and may have stepped on a few toes during her time on the town council. Half the town is afraid of her, and Jazz and I haven't decided if that's going to work for or against her. Maybe people will be too scared *not* to vote for her."

Sawyer chuckled. "Well, she doesn't scare me." Rather, she intrigued him, her steel-spined demeanor a seeming contradiction to the house she'd decorated with soft, frilly things. And she amused him, with her unexpected playful side, as well as impressing him with how much she clearly loved her kid. Sawyer had a lot of respect for mothers; the only person in his family he tried to maintain a relationship with was his mom.

"Wait a minute." Brody peered at him in the dim light of the glowing dashboard. "You like her, don't you? I thought the two of you would drive each other crazy."

Because she was admittedly bossy and he had a habit of provoking people—especially when it brought fire to a pair of unforgettable blue eyes? "Like I said, give it time."

"...AND YOU JUST *know* the bastard did this on purpose," Sierra concluded, pacing the length of Becca's living room as she ranted.

Seated on the sofa with her legs tucked beneath her, Hadley Lanier nodded, her dark ponytail swishing. Her summary of the situation was the same as Sierra's, but with significantly less cursing. "This is another lame attempt to sabotage you."

Originally, Becca had invited the two women over for a girls' night, since Marc was spending his Friday evening at dinner and a movie with the Whittmeyers. But plans for lighthearted conversation over sangria had become an impromptu strategy session now that Mayor Truitt had abruptly cut the budget for the upcoming centennial celebration.

"Emergency reallocation of funds, my ass," Sierra said, snagging her wineglass as she passed by the coffee table on her next lap. "Everyone associates you with the celebration, which means you could lose the election if people are disappointed enough with the festivities. He's manufacturing obstacles just to make you look bad."

"Let him try," Becca said calmly. The idiot had been trying to steer public opinion about her ever since January, when the paperwork had come in with enough signatures to officially qualify her as a candidate. At the Valentine's Day celebration—which she'd chaired— he'd been careful to praise the job she'd done, while vocally "worrying" that the town's needs were cutting into her family time with Marc. In an April interview with the *Cupid's Bow Clarion*, Mayor Truitt expressed his gratitude for the support of his wife and grown children, subtly undermining Becca by saying he couldn't imagine how difficult the job would be for a single parent.

In response, Becca had reminded everyone that Sheriff Cole Trent, the best sheriff in three generations, did his job successfully while raising two daughters alone. Of course, his circumstances had recently changed, now that he'd met and married Kate Sullivan, but Becca's point had been made.

"You're taking this remarkably well," Hadley said, her tone admiring. "I was so mad that on the drive over here, I was imagining far-fetched schemes to have Truitt disgraced. One of them involved costumes and code words and his ending up in a South American prison."

Becca shook her head at the younger woman. She'd wanted the librarian on her campaign because Hadley was bright and creative, but sometimes her imagination went to weird places. "We don't need elaborate schemes—"

"Code names could be fun," Sierra said.

"—when we have talent and skill," Becca finished. "Truitt is shortsighted. He can create unnecessary obstacles, but I'll look twice as good to voters when I overcome all of them."

Sierra tapped her index finger against her chin. "Only if the general populace knows about the behind-the-scenes obstacles. If *you* talk about problems that crop up, you risk sounding whiny. But the rest of us can strategically spread the word. Manuel and I make all kinds of small talk with our patients while trying to distract them from the pain of their workouts. And Kate's grandmother Joan can casually mention your committee progress at her quilting club and weekly senior-center poker games."

Becca nodded, although she temporarily lost her train of thought when she heard a vehicle engine outside.

Hadley cocked her head, her expression shrewd. "Everything okay? That's the third time tonight you've tensed when a car passed by."

"It is?" *Damn.* Becca had impressed her friends by being unfazed by Mayor Truitt's shenanigans, yet she was as high-strung as a horse during a thunderstorm when it came to the idea of her new tenant returning.

True to his word, Sawyer had been gone when she got up this morning. She had no idea when to expect him back—or if she'd even encounter him, given his private access to the attic. The big problem was that she hadn't informed the other two women of his presence. Earlier, she'd almost told them that she'd rented the room, but realized they'd ask to whom. She'd balked at admitting it was Hadley's "hot cowboy in the tight jeans."

Better get it over with it. This was Cupid's Bow. She was lucky they hadn't heard about Sawyer already.

Sierra laughed. "She's probably just listening for Marc to come home and you've found some way to turn it into a mystery."

"Actually, I was listening for my new tenant." Becca stood, giving the explanation casually as she carried their empty snack tray toward the kitchen. "I finally rented out that attic apartment. I told him he was welcome to use my kitchen for dinner, but I'm not sure when—or if—he'll be in tonight."

Both women were right on her heels as she refilled the platter with cheese, crackers and grapes.

"He?" Sierra asked. "Somehow I always imagined you with a female roommate."

Me and you both, sister. "Maybe I'll rent to a woman next. He won't be here long." Just a few weeks…although if she stayed this antsy the entire time, it was going to feel like a lot more.

"Who is he?" Hadley asked.

"A friend of Brody Davenport's. He's going to help with the centennial trail ride, and in the meantime he's writing some travel articles about—"

"Whoa!" Hadley's dark eyes were huge. "You don't mean the guy who was with Brody yesterday at The Smoky Pig?"

"Um, yeah." Becca cleared her throat. "That's him. Sawyer."

"I can't believe your luck!" Hadley said.

Frowning, Sierra leaned on the kitchen counter. "I'm not sure if this is good luck."

"Are you kidding me?" Hadley demanded. "She's got the hottest cowboy since *your* man living under her roof."

Sierra smiled faintly at the reference to her boyfriend, Jarrett, but her tone remained wary. "You guys know I love my adopted hometown." She'd moved to Cupid's Bow from Dallas almost a year ago. "But people here can be a little…old-fashioned in their thinking. The worst of them question whether a woman can do the job of mayor—which, hell, yes—and even the well-meaning worry about her juggling the demands with being a single mom. How is it going to look that said single mom is shacking up with—"

"Hey!" Becca objected.

Sierra waved her hand in an impatient gesture. "I'm not implying a damn thing. But you know how gossip flows in this town."

Faster than champagne at an open-bar wedding.

"Well, then you should introduce him to me," Hadley suggested with a cheeky grin. "If he and I are dating, it removes you from any speculation."

Sierra snorted. "Way to take one for the team."

"Okay, I'm not subtle," Hadley admitted, "but we don't all have gorgeous ranchers in our lives."

Sierra grinned. "Jarrett *is* gorgeous. And sweet. And more sensitive than he wants anyone to know." Her expression glowed. Witnesses would be able to tell from twenty paces that she was in love.

Had Becca looked like that in the early years of her marriage? When she was the happiest she'd ever been and fully expected that happiness to last the rest of her life? She drained her glass, trying not to feel bitter as she listened to Sierra joke about Jarrett's latest attempts to get her to try camping.

"He knows I'm not outdoorsy," Sierra was saying, "but the idea of cuddling in a sleeping bag with him does have merit."

"Aren't you going on the centennial trail ride?" Hadley asked.

"Nope. I'm all for celebrating the town's big anniversary, but I'm not a native. I'll celebrate from indoors with cake. And air-conditioning." She checked her watch. "Speaking of Jarrett... I told him I might be home early enough for us to watch a movie."

"A movie, huh?" Hadley smirked. "Is that what the kids are calling it these days?"

"Smart-ass." Sierra lightly shoved the other woman's shoulder. "How would I know what the kids are calling it? I'm older than you are."

As the only woman over thirty in the room, Becca rolled her eyes. "Neither of you are allowed to use the word *old.*"

"You're not much older than we are, but you're definitely wiser," Sierra said. "One of many reasons why you'll make a great mayor. Do you want to work on revamping the celebration budget? I can text Jarrett that I'll be late."

"Thanks, but no. You go home to your rancher, and let me crunch the numbers." The funny thing about Truitt trying to rattle her with a reduced budget was that *nothing* he threw at her could be as big a shock as her husband leaving and Becca suddenly finding herself the head of a single-income family. Before that were the years she'd tried to cobble together a grocery budget for a large family out of spare change from the sofa cushions and her brother's lawn-mowing money. Making do with less was her entire wheelhouse. "I'll call you guys this week after I've done some math."

Hadley grimaced. "Not to be an English-major cliché, but count me out. Slogans and speeches, I've got your back. Math? You're on your own, madam mayor."

As Sierra, who had a head for numbers, heckled the brunette about passing up an opportunity to improve her skills, they gathered up their purses and put on their previously discarded shoes. Then they said good-night, leaving Becca in the suddenly still house. She stayed so busy with Marc and her community activities that the peace and quiet was almost startling.

And then the phone rang.

My fault for not appreciating the silence while I had it. She picked up the cordless phone from the kitchen counter. "Hello."

"Rebecca?"

Becca flinched. "Mother?" Had something happened to one of her brothers or sisters? It was difficult to imagine anything short of an emergency prompting Odette to call. Becca could count on her fingers the number of times they'd spoken since she left home.

Her dad's funeral, her sister's wedding…the wheedling phone calls when Odette realized her late brother-in-law had left Becca all his money. When Becca had been pregnant with Marc, she'd reached out to her mother, but Odette had refused to take her calls, still holding a bitter grudge because her oldest child had eloped. "What's wrong?"

Her mother sniffed. "Does something have to be *wrong* for me to miss my firstborn?"

Concern for her siblings dissipated, suspicion filling the vacancy. Her mother had alternately relied on her and resented her over the years, but they'd never been close. "The last time you 'missed' me, it was because you'd run through the bulk of Daddy's life insurance settlement and wanted money."

"Rebecca Ruth, I did not raise you to be disrespectful. And taking care of children is not cheap."

What children? Everett drove 18-wheelers now, earning a living the same way their father had, Courtney was married in Oklahoma and Becca's twin brothers, Sean and Shane, ran their own auto body repair and paint shop. Only eighteen-year-old Molly still lived at home. There were moments Becca suffered pangs of guilt for not maintaining a relationship with her little sister, but the age gap between them didn't leave them with much in common.

Is that the real reason you haven't made more of an effort? Or are you just selfishly reveling in your freedom? Becca had given so much of herself to her siblings for so long that her relationship with her family had felt parasitic by the time she left home. Was it selfish to distance herself from them, or simply an act of self-preservation?

Even these few moments on the phone with her mother were draining her. She sagged into a kitchen chair. "You're not much older than we are," Sierra had said. But sometimes Becca felt ancient. Being forced into a caretaker role at four years old aged a woman before her time.

"I've had a long day," Becca said. "How about we get straight to the reason you called?" She spared a glance at the digital clock above the stainless steel stove. Would she have enough time to squeeze in a bubble bath before the Whittmeyers brought Marc home? But then her mind strayed to Sawyer and when he might return. The idea of being naked except for a layer of scented bubbles with the cowboy in the house made her feel oddly vulnerable. *That's ridiculous. Are you planning not to bathe or change clothes while he's staying here?* Still…

"It's about your sister," Odette said with an aggrieved sigh. "Molly's been out of high school since January, and all she's managed to do is get fired from three jobs and date two inappropriate men. The one who just dumped her is almost forty! Bet she'll go running back to him if he calls. She did last time."

Becca's stomach clenched, regret burning like an ulcer. Molly had always had good grades, nearly as good as Beccca's had been, and she'd earned enough credits to graduate a semester early. *Maybe if we'd kept in better touch, I could have helped her develop some ambition for college.* Or for anything. Knowing Odette, Becca guessed she'd been leaning on her youngest as live-in help, so why would she foster Molly's desire to leave?

It sounded as if mother and teen weren't getting

along. On the one hand, discord between them might finally motivate Molly to seek greener pastures. But Becca wanted to see her sister in community college or IT courses or dental hygienist school—*something* productive—not shacked up with a man twice her age because she didn't have the income to live on her own.

"She's impossible," Odette complained. "I don't know what the hell I'm supposed to do with her."

Parent her. But there was no point in saying that. For all that Odette had given birth to six of them, she'd never been overly invested in raising children. In fact, Becca was almost surprised her mother even cared enough to seek guidance over Molly's behavior. "Have you talked to Courtney to get her input?" Becca's second-youngest sibling knew Molly a lot better than she did.

"The situation is beyond 'input.'"

"But… I thought you were calling to ask my advice?"

"Typical. You're hoping to mumble a few parenting tips, then wash your hands of us. Is that it?"

The seething accusation in her mother's voice might have wounded Becca if she hadn't built up an immunity over the years. Odette had used the same tone when she'd labeled Becca a spoiled ingrate for going away to college when her family needed her. She'd used it when she asserted that Becca had eloped out of spite— never mind that it had been a financial decision—and again when Becca had refused to turn over her inheritance from her uncle. Odette had called her a heartless miser who'd let her family starve rather than share her windfall.

"I don't need advice," her mother said now. "I need you to look after your sister."

"No." The rush of anger was dizzying, and Becca grasped the edge of the table as her blood pressure soared. "I'm not your unpaid babysitter anymore. I'm a grown woman with my own child and a mayoral campaign who—"

"I bet you have all those Cupid's Bow voters conned into believing you value family."

Becca had too much self-control to hang up on anyone…but just barely. "If *you* value family, talk to your daughter. Molly's young. There's time for her to get her life on track before she makes an irreparable mistake."

"You be sure to tell her that when she gets there."

"When she gets here?" Becca echoed, praying she'd heard wrong.

"I was calling as a courtesy. She's probably on a bus by now. Hateful girl told me to go to hell, declared she was moving in with you, and stormed out. The two of you should get along great." And with that, her mother disconnected.

Becca sat frozen, barely registering the unpleasant buzz of the dial tone. Was Molly *really* coming here, or had she given Becca's name as a decoy because she didn't want their mother to know where to find her? Considering how long it had been since the two sisters had spoken, it seemed more likely that Molly would crash with a friend or one of those "inappropriate men" Odette had mentioned.

The sound of a vehicle in the driveway finally spurred Becca into motion. She put the phone back on its charger cradle and went to look out the window, expecting to see Sawyer. Despite her conflicted feelings about the man, at the moment she'd welcome a distraction. But it was the Whittmeyers.

She walked out barefoot to meet them. "I wasn't expecting you for another hour at least," she told her son as he hopped out of the minivan.

Lyndsay Whittmeyer rolled down her window, her Texas-sized blond curls filling the frame. "The movie was sold out, so we drove to Turtle for a round of minigolf and then brought him back."

"It's probably just as well," Becca said. "Now he can get plenty of rest before his game in the morning." They were scheduled to play at nine, which meant arriving at the soccer fields by eight thirty.

"Kick the other team's butts," Kenny called from inside the vehicle.

Marc laughed even as he cast a cautious look at Becca to make sure she didn't object to *butts. Not tonight, kiddo.* Between Mayor Truitt's pettiness and having to talk to her mother, Becca found her mental vocabulary was a bit more colorful than usual.

She was making sure her son had remembered to thank the Whittmeyers for taking him along when a taxi pulled up behind them, blocking their exit from the driveway. For years, there hadn't been any cab service in Cupid's Bow, but Arnie Richmond had decided he could make good money driving inebriated patrons home from the local bars on the weekends. Had Sawyer and Brody gone out drinking?

But it wasn't the tall cowboy who climbed out of the backseat. A curvy redhead emerged, barely topping five foot three in her boots. She glanced around nervously as Arnie popped open the truck, but then she locked gazes with Becca and smiled.

Becca blinked. "Molly?" The young woman might not have gotten much taller since they'd last seen each other, but she'd definitely grown up. The interior light from the cab showed that the tips of her sister's layered bob were streaked magenta and electric blue. And she filled out her black halter top in a very adult way.

Molly took a gigantic camo duffel bag from Arnie, handing him a crumpled wad of bills in exchange, then turned back to Becca. "Hiya, sis. Long time no see."

Chapter Five

Becca felt dazed, moving on autopilot as she waved
goodbye to the Whittmeyers and ushered her sister
up the porch steps. She managed an absent "You remember your aunt Molly?" to Marc, even though she
doubted he would. It seemed only yesterday that Becca
had been applying bandages to Molly's scraped up, preschool knees. Now her sister was a woman in painted-
on jeans and high-heeled boots.

"You look...good," Becca said diplomatically. Beneath the foyer chandelier, her sister's heavy-handed
makeup looked a little garish, but the teenager was still
beautiful. Besides, Becca had too much guilt over their
estranged relationship to open with criticism.

"Mama always said I look like you. The redhead
part, maybe." Molly's laugh was self-conscious. "Definitely not the height." She dug inside her purse and
pulled out a green pack of bubble gum. "Want one?"
she offered Marc, as she unwrapped a piece for herself.

He nodded eagerly.

"You okay with sour apple?" she asked. "I've also
got grape, watermelon and fruit pun—"

"I'm sure sour apple will be fine," Becca said.
"Marc, why don't you put on your pajamas and watch

a DVD in my room? I need a few minutes to catch up with Aunt Molly."

"'Kay, Mama. Thanks for the gum."

"Sure thing, kid." As he took off toward the staircase, Molly smiled after him. "He's cute. I always wanted a little brother. Thought it might be fun not to be the baby of the family."

Being the oldest was no picnic, either. "You're definitely not a baby anymore. You're a grown woman who gets to make adult choices. Like leaving home, apparently."

Molly's face flushed. "About that…"

"Odette only called fifteen minutes ago. The bus must have made good time."

"I decided to save the money I would've spent on the ticket and bummed a ride from a couple of guys headed in this general vicinity. We parted ways at a bar just outside town."

"*Please* tell me these were guys you knew." Becca had an appalling mental image of her sister hitchhiking on the freeway.

"Uh, it was more like a friend-of-a-friend thing," she said evasively. "But since I'm not twenty-one, I couldn't go into the bar for dinner. You got anything to eat?"

"Come on, I'll fix you a sandwich."

Molly followed slowly, studying her surroundings. "This place sure looks different than back home." There was an edge to her voice. Jealousy? Disapproval? Had she subscribed to Odette's claims that Becca should be doing more to financially assist her family? "Is there a guest room?"

What was Molly's backup plan in case there wasn't—sleeping on the sofa? "Yes."

Her sister looked away, blowing a green bubble that popped loudly. "I know you and I don't talk much, but I can't afford to get all the way to Oklahoma to stay with Courtney. Can I stay here?"

The inevitable question. Becca didn't want to think about where Molly would end up if she said no. "You can stay. But there are a few house rules and conditions."

Molly's gaze hardened. "I don't need you telling me what to do."

"You just showed up in the middle of the night on my doorstep, courtesy of a few 'friends of friends' who only got you close enough to call a cab, so maybe you should keep an open mind about sisterly advice. What do you have to lose?" Instead of waiting for an answer, she went to the refrigerator. Molly might be more amenable to guidance with food in her stomach. "I can do a bacon, lettuce and tomato sandwich or grilled cheese." She eyed a small container of leftover chili. "Or nachos."

"Grilled cheese. Courtney used to make me that with tomato soup."

And I used to make it for Courtney. It had been one of Becca's go-to dinners because the local supermarket often had canned soup as a buy one, get one free special. These days, there was soup in the house only when Marc got a cold and she cooked homemade chicken noodle. "I could heat you up a cup of chili with your sandwich."

"Just the sandwich is fine."

Silence stretched out while Becca buttered slices of bread. "You want to tell me about your fight with Odette?" she prodded.

"It wasn't my fault! You must know how unbearable she is. Everyone says you couldn't wait to get out of there."

"I got out of there with a plan—and a college scholarship. Maybe you need a plan, too." Or at least opportunities. Becca knew of a few places that were hiring in Cupid's Bow; none of them were particularly glamorous, but they didn't require specialized skills, either. If Molly was only able to find part-time work, maybe she could also do some volunteering. Becca pondered options as she flipped the sandwich in the small frying pan. Volunteering in the community would allow Molly to make contacts, while keeping her out of trouble.

"Dwayne and I had a plan. He plays guitar and I sing. We were gonna save up bus fare and an apartment deposit, go to Nashville and get famous. But then he got back together with his ex-wife. Maybe they'll break up again."

Becca wasn't sure which to address first, the statistically unlikely odds of "getting famous" or the inadvisability of fickle lovers. "First piece of sisterly advice? Don't make your plan dependent on a guy."

"What happened to your man? Mama cackled some about your getting taken down a peg, but never said why you divorced."

Becca sucked in a breath. Odette had *laughed* over it?

Given some of the things her mother had said directly to her, that shouldn't come as such a hurtful surprise. Turning off the stove, she reminded herself of the positives in her life. "The divorce represents my past. What's important is my future, raising Marc and winning this mayoral race. What do you see in *your* future?"

"Dunno. Guess I'll figure it out as I go along."

"Something smells good down here."

Sawyer! Preoccupied by the arrival of her sister, Becca had stopped listening for his return. She whirled around to find him hatless, his hair a shaggy yet somehow appealing tangle, with his chambray shirt unbuttoned over a white T.

He flashed an apologetic smile. "Didn't meant to interrupt, just wanted to grab a quick bite."

"And who might you be?" Molly asked, her eyes wide with interest. "I didn't know Becca was involved with anyone."

Becca shook her head emphatically. "Our only involvement is the rent he pays me for the apartment upstairs."

"Oh." With that breathy proclamation, Molly rose from her chair and sidled closer to him. Her attraction to Sawyer was even less subtle than Hadley's ogling yesterday.

Becca's stomach tightened as she wondered uncomfortably if the attraction would be mutual. The heavy makeup Molly wore obscured her age—assuming Sawyer was even looking at her face and not the cleavage revealed by the clingy halter top.

"Sawyer McCall, ma'am. Pleasure to meet you."

As he shook Molly's hand, Becca slapped the plated grilled cheese on the table. "Sawyer, this is my sister… my *teenage* sister."

Molly glared. "I'll be nineteen in a month. That makes me practically twenty."

No, that makes you practically nineteen. Sawyer

could date whomever he wanted—assuming she was a legal adult and didn't show up at breakfast—but Becca refused to sit idly by and watch her sister pursue another doomed liaison.

"Molly Baker." Her voice was a purr as she smiled up at him. "I'm staying here, too, so we're neighbors. Guess we'll be seeing a lot of each other."

He stepped back, softening the retreat with a smile. "You know what? After a hot day in the pasture, it was just bad manners for me to come down without showering first. Apologies, ladies. I'm going to get cleaned up."

Becca was half-afraid her sister would offer to wash his back for him, but he left the room without giving her the chance.

The minute his boots hit the stairs, Molly's smile disappeared. "You went out of your way to make me sound like a little kid!"

"I made you sound like exactly what you are. Besides, didn't we talk about how you need goals that don't include a man?"

"I'm not divorced and cynical, like you." Molly dropped back into her chair. "*I* believe in true love."

And you expect to find it with a drifter rodeo cowboy at least a decade older than you? "I'm not saying love doesn't exist. I just believe in making smart choices."

"You think I'm stupid?"

"Of course not. You did great in school. I think you can do anything you set your mind to. You just need a plan." A logical approach to life, without taking rides from strangers and throwing herself at men she'd met seconds ago.

"How would you know what I need? You barely know me."

"Well, I guess it's about time we fix that. Tonight we can—"

"My day was very draining," Molly said, her expression mutinous. "I'm going to turn in early."

"No problem." Actually, that gave Becca longer to strategize. "Tomorrow, after Marc's soccer game, we'll talk."

When her mother had called earlier, Becca had been furious that Odette was once again dumping the job of parenting on her. But, truthfully, Becca regretted not being a better sister to her youngest sibling. Starting tomorrow, she would make up for it. Becca was goal-oriented, and now she had a new goal to add to the running list: help Molly turn her life around.

WHEN YOU WERE trying to set a good example for a child—not to mention demonstrate your moral fiber to a townful of voters—you rarely indulged in vices. Becca didn't smoke, rarely swore in front of others, kept her alcohol consumption to a minimum and hadn't had sex in years. But everyone had at least one weakness. She had never been able to resist the tart temptation of key lime pie.

The one downstairs in the refrigerator was currently calling to her.

It was after midnight, a terrible time for extra calories. The smart decision would be to go back to sleep. But her sleep hadn't been restful, anyway. She'd bounced through a chaotic tangle of dreams that were half make-believe and half memory. Having Molly here had not only dredged up Becca's childhood, it reminded her how much she'd adored her father. He'd been on the road constantly, trying to provide for his family, but the days when he'd come home had been like Christmas and birthdays and the Super Bowl rolled into one, cause for Texas-sized celebration.

Even Odette, who spent hours in bed with nausea when she was expecting and fatigued headaches between pregnancies, had got excited about his return, emerging from her room with bright eyes and a warm smile that gave Becca temporary hope her mother would change. But when he left, the brightness faded. And after he'd died? The only light she'd ever glimpsed in her mother was permanently extinguished. Odette was a bitter woman with a martyr complex, always complaining about how her children didn't appreciate her.

Am I turning bitter?

Only a few hours ago, Molly had characterized her as a cynic whose worldview was tainted by divorce. Logically, Becca knew better than to let that upset her. Yet she was bothered enough to reach for the stained-glass lamp on her nightstand. Screw all this tossing and turning—life would look better after a slice of key lime.

Rather than turn on the hall light and risk disturbing Marc or Molly, Becca used the thin beam of her cell phone flashlight to guide her way downstairs. She frowned when she noted light coming from the kitchen; the fixture above the counter was on a timer and should have turned off an hour ago. Apparently, her groggy mind was too jumbled to draw the obvious conclusion—someone was in there.

It wasn't until she entered the room and met Sawyer's gaze that she belatedly made the connection. *Too late to go upstairs and pull on a robe.* There was nothing scandalous about her pajamas, but she felt a little silly in front of him—barefoot in a pink T-shirt and shorts set that was covered in pandas. He sat at the kitchen table in a thin white T-shirt and pair of faded jeans, polishing off a sandwich and a glass of milk.

"Did I wake you?" His apologetic expression gave way to a slow smile as he studied her. "Cute pj's."

She held her head high, attempting dignity as she marched to the refrigerator. "They were a birthday present from Marc. And no, you didn't wake me. I wanted a glass of water." Which sounded more mature than she'd come down to stuff her face with pie in the middle of the night. Then again, this was her damn house, and who cared what he thought of her sleepwear or her eating habits? "And pie. I *really* want pie."

"I was hungry, too. I never did get dinner earlier. Figured it would be best to let you and your sister catch up without an audience, then nodded off while checking the baseball scores. Woke up with my stomach growling. You don't mind my raiding the pantry, do you?"

"Not at all. Just, if you finish something, write it on the grocery list so I can get more." She tapped the magnetized notepad on the fridge. "And don't *ever* finish the last slice of key lime pie. I'd have to kill you in your sleep."

"Nah. You wouldn't stoop to a sneak attack. If you decided to take a man out, he'd see you coming."

"Thanks. I think." When she opened the fridge door, she saw that there was over half a pie left in the fluted dish, and turned toward him. "You want some of this?"

He arched an eyebrow, his gaze wicked. "Just to clarify what you're offering, sweetheart—"

"Oh, grow up." She should be cold from the refrigerator, not tingling with warmth over his juvenile single entendre. Slamming the door shut, she retorted, "You know perfectly well what I was—and was *not*—offering."

"Sorry," he said, with an unrepentant grin. "Did Brody warn you I have a bad habit of teasing? I made one playful comment to Jazz today at lunch, and for a second I thought he was going to come across the table. He should know better than anyone that I didn't mean anything by it."

"And *you* should know better than to flirt with other men's wives." But her tone wasn't sharp. Habitual flirt or not, Sawyer had been polite but restrained with her sister, and Becca was grateful. She carried her plate of pie to the table. "Thank you for not encouraging Molly."

"Hit on your little sister under your roof? Oh, hell, no. I'm much too afraid of you for that." He leaned back in his chair. "Besides, she's not my type."

"You don't like redheads?" Why had she asked that? Sawyer's taste in women was irrelevant, and God forbid he think she was fishing for compliments. It was not a Sensible Becca question. It was a midnight, key lime, to-hell-with-the-consequences question.

"I have nothing against redheads. I like women of all shapes, sizes, skin tones and hair colors. But getting involved with a girl that young?" He pretended to shudder, then flashed a wolfish smile. "I like experienced women."

She just bet he did. "I'm going to pretend you mean life experience."

"How do you know I didn't? There's something very appealing about a woman who's had time to figure out who she is, who knows her own mind." He held Becca's gaze, and heat prickled over her skin like a full-body blush—one she hoped was invisible.

Looking away, she reminded herself that she was not foolish enough to take his words as a personal compliment. He was a chronic charmer whose flirting, by his own admission, meant nothing. Yet the thought of a man who could appreciate a strong-minded woman was heady. Since the divorce, her few attempts at dating had shown that too many guys were looking for a female who would defer to the big strong man in her life. The guy who'd come the closest to appreciating Becca had been Will Trent, who'd taken her to dinner last December, and praised Becca's blunt, forthright nature. But she'd spent the evening exercising said bluntness and telling Will that if he had any sense, he'd win back the local florist who loved him. *And I was right.* Will and Megan had been together ever since.

Sawyer crossed the kitchen and returned with his own slice of pie. "Not that it's any of my business, but you didn't mention your sister was coming. Surprise visit?"

"Surprise doesn't begin to cover it. Molly and I haven't spoken much in the last few years."

"Is she your only sibling?"

"Hardly. There are six of us."

He gave a low whistle. "You said you could relate to my putting distance between me and my family, but that's *a lot* of family."

Hence the distance. "I love my brothers and sisters. I just didn't want to be bogged down by them." She sighed. "Is that selfish?"

"You're probably asking the wrong guy. I do what I want and go where I want and barely remember to call my mom on Mother's Day. But given how much you care about Marc and this whole town? Selfish is the last thing I'd call you."

Until he said it, she hadn't realized how much she needed to hear the reassurance. "I'm glad I rented you the attic." She grinned at him. "Despite my original misgivings, you're not completely terrible."

"Thanks. I think."

MARC SAT ON the kitchen floor, trying to pull up the bright blue socks; they were tight, because of the built-in shin guards. This was taking too long. His cereal was going to get soggy. He hated soggy cereal. One time, at Kenny Whittmeyer's house, Mrs. W let them have *cookies* for breakfast. She'd said cookies probably weren't any less healthy than doughnuts. Marc loved his mom, but no way would she ever serve cookies for breakfast.

"Morning." Mr. Sawyer walked into the kitchen, pausing on his way to the coffeepot to ask, "Whatcha doing down there?"

"I have to put on these socks."

"You sure those are socks?" Mr. Sawyer filled a coffee mug and took a sip without stirring in all the extra stuff Mama used. "They look long enough to be pants."

"They're special. For soccer." Suddenly, Marc had an idea so excellent that he forgot all about soggy cereal and how he couldn't kick the ball too good. "Do you wanna come to my game? You can cheer for my team, the Unicorns."

"The Unicorns?" Mr. Sawyer didn't say anything mean, but Marc could tell from his expression that he thought the team name was kind of dumb. "Was that your mother's idea?"

"No. Everyone on the team had to suggest an animal, and then we voted. I said T. rex, but Jodie Prescott wanted *unicorn*. I guess unicorns are okay. They're just like horses 'cept with sharp horns they can use to stab their enemies."

"I don't know much about soccer, but I think stabbing the other team is a foul."

Marc grinned, climbing up from the floor to sit at the table with his new friend.

"Afraid I can't make the game this morning," Mr. Sawyer said. "I promised to help Brody on his ranch before the day gets too hot. Do you have another game soon?"

"Oh, yeah. Tuesday." Marc had almost forgotten that he had to play a makeup game for one that got rained out. "Horse riding Sunday, piano on Monday, soccer on Tuesday." Every Wednesday, they had dinner and choir rehearsal at the church.

"Sounds like you have a pretty full week."

"Yep. On Thursday, we have soccer again. Practice, not a game." Marc dipped his spoon in the cereal. Maybe it would rain on Thursday. Practice could get canceled. *Mama would just reschedule it.*

Mr. Sawyer frowned at him. "You don't sound very enthusiastic. Do you like soccer?"

Marc glanced at the door to the garage; Mama had gone out to the extra refrigerator to get bottled water for the team. She would be back any second. "It's fine, I guess."

"Want to try that once more with feeling?"

"What?"

"Never mind." He followed Marc's gaze toward the door. "Do you not want your mom to know how you feel?"

"I…" Marc didn't want to complain about Mama. At school, there had been an assembly where the principal talked about bullying. She gave them a list of mean things they should never do, including talk "behind someone's back." Was that what he and Mr. Sawyer were doing? Marc got out of his chair and carried his bowl to the sink.

"Sorry, buddy. Didn't mean to upset you."

"I'm not upset." Marc smiled over his shoulder, the same kind of smile he gave adults when they talked about his daddy and Marc didn't want anyone to know he was sad. He didn't want to be called a crybaby; getting called Shorty was bad enough. Even though Kenny Whittmeyer was Marc's best friend, sometimes Marc got mad at him for stupid reasons—like being taller, even though Kenny couldn't help it. And not having *any* lessons after school. Kenny used to take a karate class, but Mrs. W made him stop when he kept karate chopping stuff at the house, including his big brother, Coop.

A snake, no lessons and cookies for breakfast. That was the life.

From behind him, Mr. Sawyer said, "Tell you what, I will definitely come to your game on Tuesday."

"You will?"

"Just let me know what time, and I'm there. Go, Unicorns!" He waved his hands in the air.

Marc laughed. This had been the best week since his birthday. First, Mr. Sawyer showed up. Then Aunt Molly, with her cool hair and bubble gum. If exciting surprises kept happening, soon *Kenny* might be jealous of *him*.

By the time Sawyer returned midmorning, the rain was coming down in horizontal sheets. Cupid's Bow might be well east of the infamous Texas Tornado Alley, but the town was subject to major storms that rolled in off the coast. He'd been at Brody's for only a couple hours before both men realized ranch work would be impossible today. Sawyer had decided to return to his room and work on an article, leaving the newlyweds free to enjoy their rainy afternoon.

He parked in the driveway and sprinted for the front porch, rather than go all the way around the house to his private entrance. Becca had given him keys that would work for either door. He was removing his boots beneath the wooden roof when her van pulled up alongside his truck. The driver's door opened, and a navy blue umbrella blossomed like some mutant nylon flower.

She hustled Marc beneath the umbrella, concentrating her efforts on shielding her son rather than herself. The brief distance from the van to the porch left her as soaking wet as Sawyer was. He'd been considering taking off his damp shirt and leaving it on the porch swing to dry. Not an option for Becca, whose sodden polo shirt was clinging to the lacy bra beneath. Trying not to leer, Sawyer lowered his gaze…but then stole a peek from beneath his lashes.

Damn, her curves were sexy. He'd struggled against noticing last night, when she'd been braless beneath the thin material of her pajamas, but it was impossible to miss with her clothes plastered to her lush body. Turning away, he wrung out the hem of his shirt and tried to think appropriately G-rated thoughts. She had her kid with her, for crying out loud.

He cleared his throat. "Some weather, huh? Did your game get canceled?"

"No, we had time to finish before the rain started," Marc muttered.

"We won," Becca said cheerfully. "Six to four."

"Because of Jodie Prescott," Marc said. "She made most all of our goals."

"Yep, Jodie's quite a talent," Becca agreed.

Mother and son didn't seem to be having the same conversation. Becca was radiating pleased pride; Marc sounded as if he'd be happy to never see a soccer field—or Jodie Prescott—ever again. Surely Becca had noticed that her son wasn't interested in being the next David Beckham? *None of my business*. Maybe Becca had overruled his objections because the exercise and fresh air were healthy. Marc might not like broccoli, either, but there wasn't anything Sawyer could do besides shrug sympathetically. And make himself scarce from the dinner table on broccoli nights.

Becca knelt down to untie her son's shoes and help him out of his shin guards. "You change into dry clothes as fast as you can, and I'll see if we have the ingredients for hot chocolate. Not a typical drink for May, but this isn't exactly 'typical' weather." She rose, reaching for the door. "Actually, this storm is an excellent opportunity."

Sawyer stared skeptically at the rain. "For what?" Turning the streets into canals and attracting tourists with gondola rides?

"Well, you and Brody can't get any ranch work done in *this*."

"Definitely not. Which is why I came back to—"

"And on the day I rented the attic to you, we agreed that occasional babysitting would cover your meals here."

"True. But—"

"And my sister is in desperate need of a job. The sooner she starts applying, the sooner she'll find one."

"You want to go running around town now? I hope you have a boat in the garage."

"Her willingness to seek employment in this weather will make a good impression. It demonstrates tenacity and a strong work ethic."

Molly's "willingness"? Somehow he didn't think the young woman was going to get a choice in the matter— much like Becca wasn't giving him any. Then again, he did agree to periodic babysitting. "Sure. I can watch Marc for a few hours."

"I was hoping you'd see things my way. He's not a picky eater, so lunch can be whatever's simplest to make. He's allowed one soda, as long as it's not caffeinated. Thank you, Sawyer." Becca beamed at him, her smile so approving that for a split second he felt like a hero. He would have agreed to almost anything she asked. Thankfully, instead of making more requests, she turned and went inside.

When he'd moved in, he'd told himself he could

charm his disapproving landlady into liking him. But he had underestimated *her* charm. If Becca ever realized the true power in her smiles, he might end up wrapped around her manicured little finger.

Nah, no reason to panic. He hated being told what to do. That hadn't changed. It was just damned difficult to say no to a beautiful woman in a wet shirt.

Chapter Six

The storm had not let up in the hour since Becca had loaded her scowling sister into the minivan, both of them in raincoats. If anything, the wind had increased and the thunder was growing louder. Sawyer stared out the window, trying to ignore just how uncomfortable he was with the idea of her out driving. *Since when are you a worrier?* He used to have casual conversations on the sidelines of rodeo arenas while his friends risked life and limb on the backs of fifteen-hundred-pound bulls. Becca had done just fine taking care of herself before he came along, and she didn't need his concern.

Another thunderclap rattled the house, and he turned toward the sofa, where Marc was supposedly reading a book. It had been ten minutes since he'd last turned a page. They could both use something productive to do.

"Want to help me look for candles and flashlights?" Sawyer asked. "In case the electricity goes out."

The kid frowned, his tone perplexed. "Even if the lights go out, we don't need candles. It's *daytime*."

True. Becca had said she'd be back by four, or would call if Molly had a strong lead and needed more time to interview. "You're right. Guess I'm just…" *Worried? Preoccupied by your mother? Hoping that rain-*

coat keeps her dry so no SOBs are leering at her in wet clothes? "Bored. Want to play a video game or something?"

"We don't have a console. Kenny Whittmeyer has an Xbox. Even Jodie has a PlayStation."

"Maybe you can ask for one for Christmas?" Sawyer suggested sympathetically.

Marc flopped back on the couch. "That's what Mama said, too. Do you know how far away Christmas is?"

I'll be an uncle by then. It was a surreal thought. He and Charlie used to torment each other with stupid pranks. Hard to believe that the obnoxious kid who once stuck a frog in Sawyer's boot was going to be someone's father.

Thinking about those pranks, Sawyer felt a pang of nostalgia. As much as he and Charlie had plagued each other, they'd both adhered to the unspoken rule of no tattling. They'd relied on creative revenge rather than running to their parents—and woe to anyone outside the family who messed with either of them. They were a united front against perceived enemies. *We were partners.* Equal in worth, if not age. That had changed when Charlie went to college and became the first McCall to finish his degree.

"What about a board game?" Sawyer asked. "Or cards?"

"Do you know how to play checkers?"

"It's been a while, but yeah. Want to play at the kitchen table and finish off the key lime pie?"

Marc's eyes went wide. "That's a bad idea. Key lime is Mama's favorite."

"Don't worry, buddy, I was only kidding. But I could rustle up a snack if you're hungry."

He shook his head. "Can we play out on the porch? I want to see the rain."

"The thunder doesn't scare you?" Sawyer was impressed; that was some significant weather out there.

"It used to. But Mama and I watch the lightning from the porch swing sometimes."

"Sounds good to me."

As Marc scampered off to get the checkers board, Sawyer found himself imagining what it would be like to share that swing with Becca, her soft curves cuddled against him as the two of them marveled at the pyrotechnics of a Texas storm. *Except it wouldn't be the two of us.* Becca was a package deal—and even if Sawyer's life were stable enough that he felt comfortable dating a single mom, it was difficult to believe Becca would voluntarily snuggle up to him.

Difficult, but not impossible.

Sure, she was more subtle than her sister, but that didn't mean she was indifferent. There'd been those admiring glances across the barbecue restaurant, and since then, her teasing last night and the intimate way she'd smiled at him when he'd agreed to babysit. In general, he avoided complications and bossy people. But for the chance to find out if the attraction went both ways…? *It's not like you can avoid her, anyway. You live together.* More or less.

"Found it!" Marc called. He returned, holding a battered cardboard box with masking tape around the corners.

Sawyer pushed aside indecent thoughts about Marc's mom and opened the door for the kid. "You do realize that even with the roof, we're going to get a little wet? The rain will blow onto the porch." The sound of the howling wind reverberated all around them. Wait— that noise was more than the wind.

Marc cocked his head. "Do you hear that, Mr. Sawyer?"

"Yeah." The intermittent sound wasn't exactly a howl; it was a high-pitched whine coming from somewhere in the yard below. Blinking rain out of his eyes, Sawyer leaned over the railing and saw a black-and-gold tail, stubby hind legs and a wiggling butt that suggested frantic movements from the unseen front half of the body. A small dog, probably no more than a puppy, had tried to get under the porch and appeared to be stuck in the latticework.

"That's a *dog*!" Marc was breathless with excitement, his words running together. "We have to save it."

Sawyer was already on his way down the steps. If the dog kept up its panicked struggling, it would either break the lattice or injure itself, or both. "You stay put," he told Marc, "and I'll—"

But the boy scrambled past him, jostling Sawyer, missing the bottom step and nearly landing on his face on the sidewalk before making a wobbly recovery. Sawyer's heart was in his throat as he envisioned having to tell Becca that her baby's nose was broken, yet Marc seemed unfazed by his near tumble on the concrete.

"Do you think he's okay, Mr. Sawyer? What kind of dog is it? Where did he come from? Does he have a collar?"

The kid's rapid-fire delivery gave Sawyer a better understanding of Becca's no-caffeine rule. It was easy to see what Marc would be like after downing an energy drink.

"I won't be able to tell if he has a collar on until I free him," Sawyer said, keeping his voice low so that he didn't spook the animal further. "And I won't be able to help him until you move out of my way."

Marc scrambled to the side in such haste that his shoes slid in the mud and he toppled over. He grinned sheepishly. "Oops."

Reassured that the boy was unhurt, Sawyer focused on the squirming dog. "This would be easier if you'd hold still a second," he muttered, wrapping his hands around the animal to steady him. The dog yowled in protest, but was free a moment later.

It was a German shepherd puppy, little more than a black-and-gold fur ball, with big clunky feet that hinted at his eventual size. Correction, Sawyer noted, lifting the puppy by the scruff of its neck, *her* eventual size. "It's a girl."

"She's so cute!"

"Maybe when she's dry," Sawyer said. "Right now, she's a wet, dirty mess. And frankly, so are you. We should get you inside and cleaned up before your mom gets home."

"What about the puppy? We can't leave her out in this storm!" A well-timed thunderclap punctuated Marc's words.

Sawyer stood, carrying the puppy up the stairs. No way could he bring it into Becca's house, but he and Marc should at least finish their conversation out of the rain. The kid was going to catch a cold at this rate. "Maybe I can rig up some kind of pen for her out here."

"We can't leave her out here *alone*. She'll be scared."

"She can't run loose through your house, either." Although, technically, the puppy didn't seem interested in running. Worn-out from trying to escape the clutches of the evil lattice, she was now nestled into Sawyer's body heat, her breathing a soft, growly snore.

"She can stay in *your* apartment," Marc suggested, a gleam in his eye. The hint of rebellion made him look like a completely different kid than the miserable boy Sawyer had chatted with that morning, the one who'd struggled into shin guards for a soccer game he didn't want to play.

For a moment, Sawyer considered the idea. The only things of value he had with him were his laptop and his guitar, both easily placed out of the puppy's reach. "Your mom wouldn't like it."

Marc's face fell. "No, I guess not. She doesn't like video games. Or sodas. Or sn—"

"Or snakes. I remember."

Becca liked order and rules and sending her son to a structured activity for every day of the week. Sawyer thought again of the pranks from his youth, the scrapes he and Charlie got into that had been so much fun they'd almost always been worth the consequences. He and his brother might not see eye to eye as adults, but they'd shared a hell of a childhood. Marc lived in a spotless house with pink furniture and no siblings. In the years to come, what would his treasured memories of mischief be?

"We're *only* taking the puppy upstairs to get her out of this storm," Sawyer stated, finally relenting. "And you have to bring me a towel to dry her off first. If the rain stops before your mom returns, we can ask a few of your neighbors if they're missing a dog. Her owner probably lives close by."

"What if she doesn't have an owner?"

Sawyer suddenly found himself grinning at a memory of his first day here. Becca had said she wanted a guard dog. *Careful what you wish for, sweetheart.*

"WELL, THAT WAS a *very* productive afternoon," Becca chirped, injecting as much positivity into her tone as humanly possible. Her optimism might rub off on Molly.

Eventually.

For now, Molly was sighing heavily in the passenger's seat. "Yeah, I'm sure we set some record for the most food-service forms filled out in a storm." Under Becca's supervision, she'd completed six applications, starting with one for the concessions booth at Cupid's Bow Cinema and ending at the local deli, where they'd picked up food for dinner. "Gee, do I want to serve overpriced popcorn for a living or glop mayo on people's sandwiches? Hard to pick between two dream careers."

If they'd been at home, where Becca's attention wasn't divided between conversation and the dwindling visibility as evening approached, she would have pointed out that the Reyes family, who owned the deli, were some of the town's most well liked citizens or that Molly would be *lucky* to get a call from the movie theater manager after smacking her gum through their entire conversation and answering his questions with sullen curtness. But now was not the time to provoke an argument.

"At least the movie theater job offers later hours,"

Becca commented. When Molly had opened one eye long enough to refuse an invitation to the soccer game that morning, she'd mumbled that she was more of a "night person." Becca turned her windshield wipers to their highest speed, keeping her observations conciliatory. "Whatever job you end up with now doesn't have to be a long-term career. Look at it as a stepping stone." And perhaps the necessary motivation to come up with a better plan. "If you don't want to live with me or Odette forever, you need a steady income."

"Or I could just get married."

Rainy conditions or not, Becca couldn't help jerking her gaze off the road long enough to glare at her sister. "What an appalling thing to say."

"Plenty of wives don't have jobs. Mom never did."

"But that's no reason to get married! And for the record, being a mom or dad *is* a full-time job. More than a job, actually." Such a simplistic term couldn't begin to sum up the difficulties and joys of parenting. Odette had tried to delegate away the difficulty; by doing so, how many of the joys had she cheated herself out of?

"Let me get this straight. Finding a husband was okay for you, but would be 'appalling' for me?"

"Molly, I hope you do fall in love and get married. Someday. Years from now." *And I hope it turns out a hell of a lot better than my marriage did.* "But I met Colin while I was in college. If I'd never dated him or anyone else, I still would have left the university with a degree and a plan for the future. It was my scholarship, not my marriage, that allowed me to—"

"Escape the rest of us?" There was genuine pain in her soft question.

"Molly…"

"Whatever. I get it. Must have sucked, taking care of a bunch of bratty brothers and sisters." She stared out the window. "I can barely take care of myself, right?"

As Becca turned into the driveway, she felt a twinge of cowardly relief that getting out of the vehicle would provide a convenient end to the conversation. Normally, she wasn't one for avoidance. But in this case? She didn't know what to say. Molly had her faults, but resentment toward the big sister who'd abandoned her wasn't unwarranted.

Becca couldn't resolve that, not in the next ninety seconds, but she hated for their afternoon to end on such a sour note. "You were really good with those kids at the library. I know Hadley will appreciate you volunteering a few hours a week."

Since they'd been next door to the library, Becca had dropped by to introduce her sister. In her midtwenties, Hadley might be a good role model, while being closer to Molly's age. And if Molly was sticking around Cupid's Bow for a while, she should meet people—people who weren't inappropriate men.

When the conversation had turned to the election, Molly had wandered off and helped a little girl find a book. After that, Hadley had wrangled Molly's agreement to come read stories a couple times a week.

In a perfect world, Hadley could hire Molly for a paying job, but the town library had suffered some budget cuts. If—*when*—Becca was elected, maybe she could find a way to redistribute funds. Not for her friend or her sister, but because she thought access to books was a much better priority than some of Mayor Truitt's showy pet projects.

"Thanks," Molly said. "Hadley seemed okay."

"Would you be interested in a job working with kids?" Becca asked. "There's a day care center and a preschool at the church. They aren't open on Saturdays, and I'm not sure if either is actively hiring, but we—"

"I'm hungry and I want to put my wet feet into the warmest socks I can find." Molly yanked her door open. "Maybe give the career-counselor bit a rest?" Without waiting for a response, she stomped toward the house.

That could have gone better.

Could've gone worse, too. Rather than focus on negatives, Becca decided to count today as a victory; less than twenty-four hours after arriving in town, Molly had multiple job leads and had met a potential new friend. It was a decent start.

Gathering up the bags from the deli, she followed after her sister. In the living room, Marc was lying on the floor with a deck of cards. She was surprised to find him showered and in his pajamas before dinner. After setting the food on the kitchen counter, she returned, leaning down to kiss the top of Marc's head, breathing in the apple scent of his children's shampoo and marveling at how fast her little boy was growing. "Hey, champ. What are you up to?"

"Trying to build a house out of cards. Mr. Sawyer showed me earlier, but I'm not very good."

"Not yet, but that's why we practice, right? Where is Mr. Sawyer?"

"Why?" Marc's gaze jerked to her face, then slid away. "Do you need him? He went upstairs when we heard you and Aunt Molly outside. We probably shouldn't bother him. He might need some alone time.

Mrs. Whittmeyer is always sending Kenny and his brother and his dad camping so she can have 'alone time.'"

Becca laughed. "Yes, well, the Whittmeyer boys can be a handful. Did you give Mr. Sawyer any trouble?"

"I was real good. I read my book and took a shower."

"So I noticed. It's a little early for pj's. Tired after soccer this morning?"

"No. But my clothes were dirty. F-from playing checkers with Mr. Sawyer!"

She had to remind him to bathe after horseback-riding lessons and soccer practices, but he found the condition of his clothes unacceptable after a checkers match? "I didn't realize checkers was such a rough-and-tumble sport."

"So there's a full-contact version?" Molly leaned against the doorjamb, standing on one foot as she peeled off a damp sock. "I'll have to ask Sawyer to teach me."

Becca shot a quelling glance at her sister. *You, behave.* Her cell phone rang and she saw that Kate Trent was calling, probably about the festival, which kicked off a week from tomorrow. She left the room to take the call.

Kate didn't bother with a hello. "Parade emergency!" Her voice was tremulous, unlike the calm, patient tone she used when teaching Marc's piano lessons. "The roof of Jed Harker's decrepit barn collapsed."

"Oh, God, is he okay?"

"No one was in it. But he was storing three floats for us."

Becca knew that the local fire department had offered Jed money in the past for the barn, wanting to burn it down as a training exercise. It was not exactly a shock that the building had fallen apart. She was just glad no one had been hurt. "I'll go through the festival phone tree and put together a list of people who can help repair floats—"

"At least one of them is beyond saving. Completely destroyed!"

"People who can help build floats," Becca amended, "and I'll get back to you tomorrow night. Don't panic. We still have a week before the festival."

"Right. Of course you're right. I don't know why I got so emotional about a few parade floats."

Becca grinned, glad her friend couldn't see her knowing expression. She had a pretty good idea why Kate had been so emotional lately—and why, green faced, the sheriff's wife had suddenly bolted from the campaign meeting Thursday, claiming that the barbecue hadn't agreed with her. Did Kate not yet realize she was pregnant again, or were she and Cole waiting until the second trimester to share the news?

"The floats are under control," Becca promised. "You've done a great job coordinating the parade."

"Thank you," Kate said, finally sounding like herself. "Your notes from last year were so organized that it's been easy. Except for this slight building-caving-in hiccup."

"I'll call around and look for new places to store the floats. Structurally sound edifices only, I swear. Meanwhile, why don't you relax and get that handsome husband of yours to rub your feet or something?" Hanging up the phone, Becca realized that it felt like a different lifetime since she'd romantically pursued Cole Trent—not that romance had been her motivation exactly. After the divorce, trying to date him had seemed sensible, another case of being goal-oriented. He was a good father, a good person and good-looking. With her being on the town council and him being the sheriff, they would have been the Cupid's Bow version of a power couple. It could have canceled out her feelings of failure.

But as soon as Kate had entered the picture, Becca had been able to admit Cole wasn't the right man for her. *My own husband wasn't the right man for me, either.* Was there a right man for her? As she'd told Molly, a strong, independent woman didn't need a man. Oh, but there were times she wanted one.

Focus. She had a sister to rehabilitate, a festival to run and an election to win. *But first, dinner.* Since the deli had done most of the work, all that was left was some mixing and reheating. As she pressed buttons on the microwave, she thought she heard a strange sound over the beeps and the ongoing white noise of the rain. It had been sharp and high-pitched. Some kind of animal, maybe?

She tilted her head, waiting to see if it came again. But other than the muffled sound of Sawyer's footsteps two stories above, there was nothing. Obviously just something outside. Or maybe the cowboy was watching the Discovery Channel and had the volume up too loud.

Dismissing her curiosity, she did a mental run through of centennial events. The official kickoff was Sunday morning. She, as festival chairperson, would give a brief welcome address in the downtown gazebo, followed by a speech from Mayor Truitt. She would attempt to not publicly roll her eyes while he was talking. Then came the parade.

Sunday night was her big triumph, the sold-out concert that was drawing in tourists from neighboring regions. She'd called in a favor and booked a young woman originally from Cupid's Bow who'd won a reality TV singing contest a few years ago; thinking of the girl's resulting celebrity made Becca feel guilty that she'd been so quick to dismiss Molly's hope of musical fame. But—

There! It was that same sound as earlier. And it definitely hadn't come from outside.

Marc came around the corner in a hurry. "Hey, Mama—"

"No running in the house," she reminded him. "Did you hear that noise?"

"Wh-what noise? I didn't hear a noise. That's not why I came in here! I'm hungry. That's why I came to the kitchen. Is it time for dinner?"

"Pretty much." Her son was acting squirrelly. "Want to set the table while I go tell Sawyer we've got food ready?"

"No!"

"Marc Paul, what on earth is going on?"

"N-nothing. But remember about his alone time?"

"Did he specifically say he needed to be left alone?" She wanted to know what Sawyer was up to and exactly how he'd spent the hours he was supposed to be watching her son.

"No." Marc hung his head, not meeting her gaze. "But...what if he's taking a nap?"

"I heard lots of movement up there. Don't worry, he isn't asleep." Before her son could suggest any other obstacles, she marched up the first flight of steps.

Above her, she heard the door to the attic apartment

open and close. Sawyer met her halfway down the spiral staircase, moving so quickly it was on the tip of her tongue to tell *him* not to run in the house; they almost collided in the narrow space.

"Hi." His smile was casual, as if there was nothing odd about him barreling down the steps like a one-man stampede. "How'd it go with your sister?"

"Not bad." She'd need to move in order for him to come down the rest of the way, yet she stood where she was, peering past him, unable to shake the feeling that he was hiding something. "How did it go here?"

"Great."

"Are you sure? Because Marc is—"

A sharp bark interrupted her, followed by a long, plaintive howl.

Sawyer scrubbed a hand over his face. "I can explain."

Chapter Seven

From the way Becca's eyes narrowed to accusing slits and the delicate flare of her nostrils, Sawyer half expected her to shove him down the stairs. He had the height and weight advantage, but fury could provide an adrenaline boost. *This is what I get for ignoring Brody's warnings. Hope he takes good care of my truck.*

But when Becca struck out with one hand, it was only to nudge him to the side as she tried to squeeze past. It didn't work. They ended up wedged in the stairwell together. Under the circumstances, he probably shouldn't be enjoying it so much, but her angry breathing exaggerated the rise and fall of her breasts under her shirt and she smelled so good...

"You smuggled a dog into my house?"

"I temporarily sheltered a puppy in need."

She angled her hips to slip free. The wiggle was pleasant to watch, as was the view as she stomped up the remaining stairs. "What if it chews up my attic while you're eating dinner with us? Did you even think about that? And how dare you encourage my son to be dishonest! What kind of example is that setting for Marc and Molly?"

It was your son's idea. But no self-respecting man

blamed a seven-year-old. "You do realize Molly is technically an adult and not an impressionable child who needs to be protected?"

Apparently, that was the wrong thing to say, because Becca blasted him with a fulminating glare over her shoulder as she opened the attic door.

After lining the floor with copies of the *Cupid's Bow Clarion* from the recycling bin and removing everything he could from her reach, Sawyer had put the puppy in the small bathroom with a bowl of water. Now she was pawing frantically at the bathroom door, whining at their approach. The moment Becca turned the doorknob, the shepherd launched herself forward, running in circles as she yipped.

Shaking her head, Becca scooped up the dog. "I should've expected you."

"You recognize her?" That made sense. As he'd told Marc, the puppy probably belonged to a neighbor.

"No." Trying to shush the dog, Becca sat in the nearby chair. "But they say trouble arrives in threes. First you. Then Molly. This just makes sense."

Had she just compared Sawyer to some kind of dark omen? "Hey! I thought you decided you like me."

"Doesn't mean you aren't trouble."

Smart woman. "On a scale of one to I'm evicted, how ticked off are you about the dog?"

"I don't mind that you brought her in out of the storm. What kind of monster do you think I am? But letting Marc think it's okay to lie—especially when you both so clearly suck at it—was pretty crappy of you."

He should be regretting that, not watching her fingers stroke the dog's coat, noting that Becca was naturally affectionate and wondering what it would take to coax some of that physical affection his way. "So, uh, you really haven't seen her before?"

"Nope. And I don't know of anyone in the neighborhood who owns a German shepherd. I can ask around and put up signs, but if no one claims her..." She scratched behind the puppy's ear. "What am I supposed to do with you, trouble?"

"You can't call her that. You'll give her a complex."

"Yeah." She studied the dog, sprawled on her back with her paws in the air and tongue lolling out to the side. "I can see she's distraught." After a moment, Becca cast a sidelong glance in Sawyer's direction. "Will it give you a complex if I call *you* trouble?"

"Nah, I'm tough. Unless you're attracted to vulnerable, sensitive men. In which case..." Pressing a palm to his heart, he did his best to look wounded.

She chuckled, but there was an endearingly self-conscious undertone to her laugh. "I don't—"

"Hey!" Molly's voice reached them before she actually made it to the top of the stairs and poked her head in the room. "You two are taking a long time up here. Marc was worried. He sent me to make sure you hadn't 'kicked out Mr. Sawyer.'" She blew a purple bubble as she surveyed the situation. After it popped, she said, "Cute dog. Are y'all coming downstairs or what?"

Becca nodded. "We'll be there in a minute. And you can assure Marc that I'm not tossing Mr. Sawyer out into the street." She shot him a warning glance. "Not tonight, anyway."

SAWYER WAS NOT surprised that dinner conversation revolved around the puppy. Rather than leave the dog upstairs, unhappily alone, Becca had fashioned a makeshift crate out of a large laundry basket lined with old towels. After wolfing down a few bites of the chicken Becca pureed in the food processor, the puppy curled up and slept in a corner of the kitchen.

"What if we can't find her owner?" Marc asked eagerly.

Feeling delayed guilt about how he'd handled the situation, Sawyer tried to intervene before the kid started pressuring Becca to keep the dog. "I'll bet Cupid's Bow has an animal shelter of some kind. Maybe she could stay there until someone adopts her into a good home."

Becca clapped a hand to her forehead. "Oh, that'll go over *great*. Truitt can paint me as a heartless woman who dumped a puppy at the pound. How can I convince voters I can take care of our town if I can't take care of a single dog?"

Sawyer hadn't quite thought of it that way. "We might still find out where she belongs. And if not... maybe she can help you in the election. There's a long tradition of political pets. Hell, wasn't there some book about a dog in the White House?"

"Mr. Sawyer," Marc said in a loud whisper, "we don't say *h-e-l-l*."

"Right. Sorry." Trying to coax a smile from Becca, he added, "Who knows? Maybe adopting Trouble could be your first step on the path to global domination. Today, Cupid's Bow. Tomorrow, the world."

Molly giggled, but Becca just rolled her eyes. "All I need is Cupid's Bow, thanks. That's the difference between me and Truitt. He bases too many decisions on what might advance him to 'bigger things.' I'm not trying to launch a political career, I just want to do right by this town."

It was apparently something she felt strongly about because twenty minutes later, when Molly and Marc had taken the puppy outside and Sawyer was handing Becca containers of leftovers to put in the fridge, she was still discussing her plans. Plans she insisted were for the good of the citizenry, not for her own selfish benefit.

"Take the community center, for example." Shoving the small box of potato salad onto the shelf with enough force that it toppled over, she launched into a detailed accounting of the town budget. She lamented about services she felt Truitt was willing to overlook in favor of new, splashy efforts that got him more press—and possibly more votes. "By his logic, why even have the children's library, right? Kids can't vote. And his attitude toward the senior center—I mean, most of those men and women have lived in Cupid's Bow for decades. They *made* this town! For him to…"

Sawyer gamely tried to listen, but it was easy to get lost, staring at her expressive mouth, appreciating the fire in her eyes, watching her body bounce and sway as she gestured for emphasis.

She stopped abruptly, blowing out a breath. "I ranted for too long, didn't I? See, this is why I need Hadley to help me prep for speeches. So no one thinks I'm boring."

"You aren't boring. You're…passionate." His tone was more intimate than he'd intended. Consciously, he'd only meant to signal encouragement. But subconsciously, he had been mentally replaying the image of her in that wet shirt all afternoon…

Blinking, she leaned against the refrigerator door, uncharacteristically speechless. When she found her voice, it was soft, questioning. "Look, if this is my imagination running amok, tell me to get over myself, and I won't bring it up again. But upstairs, joking about me being attracted to you, and just now... Are you flirting with me?"

Busted. He grinned sheepishly. "Not very well, if you have to ask. Want to give me pointers?"

Her mouth quirked in an attempted answering grin, but she smoothed it away with a shake of her head. "I'd be flattered, if you hadn't already admitted that you flirt with every woman—teenagers notwithstanding. Regardless, it isn't a good idea. Things could get... complicated between us. You live here."

"Which means I'm conveniently located."

"Sawyer! Be serious. I have a very full plate—and a kid—and you'll be gone from Cupid's Bow in, what, two weeks? Two and a half? So never mind what kind of man I find attractive. Or how..." her gaze slid away "...passionate I am."

"So this is a bad time to ask you out?" At her glare, he raised his palms in front of him. "Kidding! I was kidding." But only because he already knew the answer would be no. Whatever else could be said about her, Becca was beautiful and smart and kept him on his toes. There were far worse ways to spend two and a half weeks than in her company. "I'm going to retreat upstairs and quit hassling you. Want me to take the puppy back up with me?"

"Are you going to keep her? Take her with you when you leave Cupid's Bow?"

"Hadn't planned to." He liked dogs, but he was on

the move a lot. The cab of his truck didn't seem like the best environment for a puppy.

"That's what I thought. She can sleep in my room. Tomorrow, I'll try to find where she came from, and if that doesn't pan out, I guess I'm now the proud owner of a German shepherd."

He winced. His impulsive decision this afternoon may have landed her a pet for the next decade. Sawyer was unaccustomed to thinking long-term. The closest he'd come was investing in prize-winning livestock, because he'd known he wouldn't be able to ride forever. And even then, someone had approached him with the opportunity. "I guess it's good you're a dog person."

"I never said that. I…implied it, but I was fibbing." She sighed heavily. "Marc's wanted a pet for a long time, though, and Trouble's young, so she can be trained without my having to overcome years of bad habits. I'll work everything out."

"Undoubtedly." The people of Cupid's Bow would be fools not to vote for her. As far as he could tell, she calmly and logically overcame every problem thrown her way—from divorce to unemployed siblings to surprise canines. "I hope it's not too flirty to pay you one last compliment? You're about the most capable woman I've ever met, Becca Johnston."

That earned him a real smile, a wide curve of generous lips he deeply regretted not being able to kiss. "Even if it was flirting, maybe I'll overlook it. Just this once."

SUNDAY WAS PROVING to be a mixed bag. Becca's attempts to determine where Trouble had come from were futile—with each passing hour, it became clearer that she was now a dog owner. *Yippee.* But in the win column, the manager of the Cineplex called during lunch to offer Molly a job. Becca hoped her sister showed more gratitude in person than she did while on the phone.

Molly was scowling as she rejoined everyone at the table. "I'll have to wear a uniform."

So? Was she afraid the vest with the movie theater logo on it would be less flattering than the men's shirt she currently wore with ripped shorts? Becca shoved a forkful of salad in her mouth to keep from commenting. She darted a glance in Sawyer's direction, recalling how he'd laughed when he discovered she was running for mayor. *See? I can be tactful.* Sort of.

"He said to be there by three," Molly added, "so he can show me the ropes before it gets busy tonight. Can I borrow your mom-mobile?"

Becca hesitated. Lend her only vehicle to the young woman who'd been impatient for Becca to speed up during yesterday's storm, even though road conditions were dangerous?

"I'm a good driver. Shane and Sean taught me a ton about cars." Molly had been the twins' receptionist at their auto body shop for six weeks before it became apparent that three Bakers under one roof made for a tense working environment. As far as Becca could tell, that had been the start of her sister's downward career spiral.

"It's not a question of your driving skills," Becca said. At least, it wasn't a question of *only* that.

"I could take her," Sawyer volunteered. "I was thinking about running into town, anyway. Brody says there's a tack-and-supply shop downtown. The zipper on my gear bag broke, and I need more rosin before the rodeo." He'd told Becca not to expect him for any meals on Wednesday because he was making an overnight trip to Refugio to ride in an exhibition rodeo.

Seated next to him, Molly laid a hand on his sleeve, looking far more enthusiastic about his offer than she had about being gainfully employed. "That would be *so* nice of you."

"Or we could all go together!" The words erupted out of Becca before she'd even had a chance to consider them. "I have to get puppy supplies. That's why I was reluctant to give you my car, Molly. Because I have errands to run. Why take more vehicles than we need, right?" Forcing a smile, she met her sister's irritated gaze, refusing to back down. Becca's interference was for the greater good—she would serve as a buffer between her sister and the disinterested Sawyer, keep Molly from making a fool of herself and pick up dog supplies. Which she really did need.

Her suggestion was motivated by sound reasoning. *Not* a moment of irrational jealousy at the idea of Molly alone with Sawyer and the pretty young woman undoubtedly throwing herself at him again.

"Sounds like a plan." Sawyer rose from his chair, carrying both his empty bowl and Marc's to the sink.

Her son looked absolutely thrilled. Becca wasn't sure what excited him the most, the increasing likelihood that he would get to keep Trouble or a shopping trip with his new hero.

"If we're all going to be out of the house," she told Marc, "Trouble will have to stay in the bathroom. Your job is to play with her between now and then and wear her out, so she'll take a long nap and won't feel lonely when we leave. Deal?"

"Deal!" He was already sprinting to liberate the puppy from her temporary pen.

Molly stood, too, her expression sullen and her salad unfinished.

As her sister turned to go, Becca eyed the dishes left on the table. Granted, it would take her only a moment to clean them up, but Molly needed to take responsibility for herself. "Molly, I think you forgot to rinse out your bowl." Her tone was the same polite but firm one she used when certain members of the town council refused to see sense.

Molly slowed, but didn't immediately stop. Was she going to ignore Becca and go upstairs, anyway? At the last minute, she pivoted, clearing her place and stomping to the sink, muttering under her breath the entire time.

Becca fought down her own rising temper; an argument now would just make their ride even more awkward. If such a thing was possible. A hyper kid excited about his new pet, a ticked-off teenager and a too-appealing cowboy Becca had told herself just yesterday she needed to keep a distance from—*oh, yeah, best trip into town ever.*

AWKWARD SILENCES, BECCA DECIDED, were a problem only if you didn't fill them. She used town trivia like handyman Zeke's putty, spackling over tense moments with such skill they were barely discernible.

As she steered the van into the theater parking lot, she shared the building's history, how it had been owned decades ago by a local family who showed only

G-rated films on the single screen. When the couple who owned it got divorced, the husband got the theater while the wife got their ranch and their truck. In bizarre retribution, the husband had showed only R-rated movies for a year. The town council at the time half-heartedly tried to stop him…which would have been more successful if 80 percent of the councilmen hadn't been paying customers. Eventually the single-screen theater was bought by new management and expanded into neighboring space when the drugstore moved to a different location.

"Now the theater can show three movies at a time," Becca said. It had been a big deal in Cupid's Bow when that happened. "Who knows? Maybe one day we'll go as high as five."

Sawyer grinned from the passenger seat. Marc was too engrossed in a comic book to respond and Molly had barely said a word since they'd left the house. Becca didn't appreciate the way her sister slammed the door when she exited the vehicle, but at least after she got out, the mood lightened.

Becca drove toward the downtown, continuing to highlight points of interest, from the huge gazebo in the center of town to the limited but tasty restaurant selections to the new old courthouse.

Sawyer's brow furrowed. "I'm sorry, the 'new' old courthouse?"

"The original one was built right after the town officially incorporated, in 1917. But it burned down in the eighties and they replaced it with a pink, glass-paneled monstrosity that was supposed to 'modernize' Cupid's Bow. It was damaged in the storm fallout after a hurricane a few years ago. There have been repairs since then, but the county finally decided to rebuild, honoring the area's heritage with a structure that closely mirrors the first one. So it's like the old courthouse all over again, but new."

"Huh." Sawyer sounded bemused. "Cupid's Bow is… To be honest, I'm not sure how to describe it."

"Weird," Marc chirped from the backseat. "But good weird."

Sawyer grinned over his shoulder. "There are worse things to be than 'good weird.' Thanks for the impromptu tour," he told Becca. "It's nice to get a little history before I help with the centennial ride."

"There's a lot to love here." Did she sound like a manic travel brochure? She couldn't help it. Even when she wasn't trying to fend off tense silences, she gushed about Cupid's Bow. She'd never been as attached to any place as much as she was to her adopted home. Not the blink-and-you'll-miss-it town where she'd been born or even the city where she'd gone to college. "You should check out the park when you have some free time—it's gorgeous as long as the river isn't overflowing. One of my goals if I'm elected is to have the town explore methods of flood control. Too often the park is a bog. And you have to see the old railway station before you leave town."

"Mr. Sawyer gets to see the soccer fields, too," Marc said. "At my game on Tuesday."

Becca winced at her lack of foresight. If she'd realized Marc planned to invite his new friend, she could have explained that Sawyer had his own schedule while he was in the area. As good-natured as the man was, she doubted he wanted to spend an evening watching seven-year-olds chase a ball with varying degrees of skill and team spirit. "That's a nice idea, champ, and I'm sure Mr. Sawyer appreciates the invitation, but I don't think—"

"It's okay," Sawyer said. "I promised I'd be there, and I keep my promises."

"Oh." She cut her eyes toward him, trying unsuccessfully to read his expression in too brief a time. "I hadn't realized you two already discussed it."

"That isn't a problem, is it? If I go with you?"

Yes. The more time he spent with Marc, the more the kid grew to idolize him. And the more time *she* spent with the cowboy, the harder it was to remember why she shouldn't flirt and smile and soak up his compliments.

But she'd always applauded peopled who lived up to their promises, even more so since Colin had flaked out on his marriage vows and his implied promise of raising his son. So she sounded almost sincere when she replied, "On the contrary, I'm thrilled you'll be joining us."

Sawyer waited for Marc to return his attention to reading, then lowered his voice. "This is what your 'thrilled' face looks like?" he teased softly. "Not what I would have pictured."

"I am happy you're coming with us." Happy-ish, anyway. "It just caught me by surprise."

"Me, too. I don't spend a lot of time at kids' soccer matches. But nothing's been quite what I expected since I got here."

"I know that feeling." Her life had been turned upside down for the last few days. Sawyer wasn't the only reason for the turmoil, but he was definitely at the center of it. "My life's gotten weird lately."

He grinned. "Good weird, or bad?"

"Too soon to tell." The puppy, unhappy about her confinement, had howled for part of the night, so Becca was sleep deprived, as well as frustrated by her sister's attitude. Plus, she was anxious over an upcoming debate and knew that bringing a good-looking stranger to Marc's soccer game was bound to cause whispered speculation.

Still, with sunshine streaming through the windows, her son humming cheerfully in the backseat and Sawyer smiling at her, life felt pretty damn good at the moment.

Chapter Eight

Becca didn't work at the community center on the weekends—not officially, anyway—and Monday was usually hectic. She spent it making sure rooms that had been rented out for Saturday and Sunday events had been restored to the proper condition, following up on inquiries, firming up the schedule for the coming week. This particular Monday morning was no exception, yet amid the controlled chaos, inspiration struck...with a little help from Sammy Pasek.

She was sitting at her desk in the administrative office just off the lobby when her phone rang. It was Sammy, calling between classes to ask if he could come in an hour early today in order to leave an hour sooner, to take his sister to the orthodontist. Eighteen-year-old Sammy was in a special honors program where he finished his school day early and used afternoons for volunteer service. He'd be leaving for college in August, and Becca had written him a hell of a recommendation letter.

Once she assured Sammy that the schedule change was no problem and disconnected the call, her thoughts turned to Molly. Her sister could benefit from exposure to resolute role models like Sammy. Then there was Vicki Ross, only a year or two older than Molly, who came in every Monday and Wednesday to use the weight room. Vicki's sophomore year of college had been postponed due to serious injuries she'd suffered in a car accident; she'd done physical therapy with Sierra for months. But now Vicki was healed, rebuilding her strength and planning a girls' trip with her mom to Lake Tahoe to celebrate her progress over the past year.

Becca had no point of reference for mother-daughter bonding; if she had to fly to the West Coast with Odette, she'd probably parachute out of the plane somewhere over the Grand Canyon. But that didn't mean she couldn't attempt some strategic *sisterly* bonding.

She reached for the phone, optimism welling. Granted, Molly had been annoyed yesterday when Becca hijacked her ride to work with Sawyer, but how long could the younger woman hold a grudge? A free lunch and a chance to meet some people her own age might cheer her up.

The phone rang unanswered until voice mail kicked in, so Becca hung up and tried again after updating some new rental agreements.

Finally, on her third attempt, she got an answer.

"Hello."

At least Becca assumed the greeting was "hello." The word was distorted by a huge yawn.

"Did I wake you?" Becca frowned at the clock in the corner of her laptop. It was almost eleven.

"Well, I did work last night," Molly said defensively.

"I know. I drove into town to pick you up, remember?" Becca had wanted to hear about Molly's first day, but her sister had rested her head against the window and feigned sleep until they got home. But today was a fresh chance. Better get to the reason for her call before Molly withdrew again. "I was thinking, how about I come get you and we have lunch in town together? There's an incredible barbecue place. Then you can come to the community center with me."

"Why?"

Becca hadn't expected such an incredulous response. Marc happily hung out here whenever she put in a few hours on the weekend; there were basketball courts, ping-pong tables and even a small reading nook, suggested by Hadley. "To see where I work, to introduce yourself to more of the community." She almost added "to meet a boy your own age" but was afraid it would sound judgmental. Besides, she wasn't certain whether Sammy Pasek was currently seeing anyone. "Come on, it's just a few hours," she cajoled, "and you get free food out of it."

"Fine." But the surly agreement wasn't quite as promising as Becca had hoped.

Molly's mood had not improved an hour later, when she trudged out of the house wearing enough eyeliner for all the Dallas Cowboy cheerleaders combined and a skimpy tank top, her expression daring Becca to say something.

Not walking into that trap. Her sister was about as subtle as Truitt's past attempts to publicly bait her. Besides, Molly's skin-baring fashion choices weren't *that* over-the-top for late May in Texas. People didn't take on this heat in sweater sets and slacks.

"We didn't have a chance to talk about it last night, but how was work?" Becca asked encouragingly.

"People wanted to see movies, I sold them tickets. People wanted popcorn, I filled buckets. Riveting, huh?"

Becca sighed, not objecting when her sister reached for the radio dial and filled the minivan with country music.

Luckily, not even Molly's sour mood was a match for the food at The Smoky Pig. She dug into her brisket and fries with gusto, not pausing to say much, but clearly enjoying her meal. Meanwhile, a succession of folks came over to discuss the festival with Becca. The crushed parade floats had been the first in a series of minor setbacks, but she wasn't worried. Problems were only opportunities to find solutions.

Cousins Kim and Tasha Jordan, who worked for the county EMT service and fire marshal respectively, stopped to discuss crowd control for the concert Sunday. When their order number was called at the counter, Becca bade them goodbye and turned back to see Molly looking impressed for the first time.

"You really talked Kylie Jo Wayne into doing a concert for you?" Molly asked around a bite of coleslaw.

"Well, I pleaded my case to her parents, who still live out by Whippoorwill Creek, and they eventually put us in touch. Kylie's from Cupid's Bow. She was glad to do something to give back to the community that supported her when she was on that reality show." Becca hoped she sounded modest enough, without downplaying the achievement so much that Molly lost interest. This was the first time she'd been engaged all day.

"I love her music," Molly gushed. "Do you think… do you think there's any chance you might be able to introduce me to her while she's here?"

"I honestly don't know. Her schedule will be pretty tight, and she travels with security and a manager and her band. But I promise if there's an opportunity, I will seize it."

Molly surprised her with a grin. "I believe you. You're not exactly shy."

Becca laughed. "No, I guess I'm not." Good thing. Monday night, she had a debate in town hall against the mayor, one of her last chances to officially make her case. It was on the tip of her tongue to ask Molly if she might want to come along. Would she be interested in seeing her big sister in action, or bored by the small-town politics? Before Becca had decided how to frame the question, they were interrupted by Gayle Trent, stopping by to volunteer her son Jace, in case more help was needed with float repairs.

After Gayle bustled off into the crowd, Becca realized how late it was getting. "Shoot! I'm supposed to be back in the office in ten minutes."

"Yeah, but aren't you the boss or something? No one's going to yell at you if you're late getting back."

"Maybe not, but what kind of example would I be setting for all the employees who work for me? Besides, I take pride in my work ethic. The point is to do a job well—not just well enough to avoid getting yelled at."

Molly rolled her eyes, but reached for the purse hanging on the back of her chair. "Guess we'd better head out then."

Dial it back a notch, Becca advised herself as she counted out bills for the waitress's tip. She didn't mean to sound self-righteous every time she opened her mouth, but she was trying hard to make up for lost years, time when she could have been steering Molly in the right direction. Lunch had been a start. Her sister had actually smiled at her. Hopefully, a couple hours at the community center would further the cause.

They ran into Sammy in the parking lot, and when Molly met the handsome varsity swimmer, her face lit up like the town fireworks over the Watermelon Festival. Becca tried not to grin, afraid she'd look smug about how well her plan was working. She sent the two teenagers off to the filing room with a stack of folders, and was surprised when Molly stalked back into the administrative office half an hour later, scowling. Sammy walked past not long after to help some kids retrieve a basketball that was stuck, darting a crestfallen glance in Molly's direction. She pointedly ignored him.

Should Becca broach the subject once she finished the phone call she was on?

Before she had the chance, though, Vicki Ross came into the center. When the blonde stopped to fill out the sign-in sheet for the weight room, Becca introduced her to Molly.

Vicki grinned at the magenta and blue streaks that framed Molly's face. "I like your hair. My family would probably lose their collective minds if I did something like that."

Doubtful. In Becca's opinion, the Ross family was so happy to have Vicki healthy and whole again, they wouldn't blink if she shaved her entire head and tattooed her face.

But Molly was nodding, her expression empathetic. "Family members can be super judgy." She cut her gaze toward Becca.

Trying to help someone find their footing wasn't the same as judging them. Mentally rolling her eyes,

Becca returned to her desk. The girls talked for a few more minutes, then Vicki asked if Molly wanted to be her spotter in the weight room.

When Sammy poked his head into the office to update Becca on an equipment delivery, he looked disappointed not to find Molly with her. He leaned against the door frame, not meeting Becca's gaze. "Did, uh, your sister say anything about me?"

"Like what? Did something happen?" Becca's protective instincts rose. She wouldn't have thought Sammy was the type to make a move on a girl he'd just met, but if he—

"I don't know," he said miserably. "We were talking about the pool and how she hasn't been yet." Cupid's Bow had a very nice aquatic complex, funded years ago by a donation from an oil tycoon. "And I mentioned my swim scholarship. I didn't mean to brag, but I, uh, wanted to, you know, impress her. Maybe it sounded too obnoxious? She suddenly stormed out. I'm real sorry if I made her mad."

From what Becca knew, she would have expected her sister to be flattered that Sammy wanted to impress her. "I'll mention that you apologized, but honestly, I wouldn't worry too much about this. She may have been in a bad mood because of something completely unrelated to you. Now, can you go check all the thermostats? I want to make sure the air-conditioning units are working properly after those repairs last week."

"Yes, ma'am."

Today was the start of a brand-new class in wood carving. Becca was in the lobby giving directions to a group of retired gentlemen who'd looked lost, when

Vicki Ross strolled toward the exit, whistling cheerfully.

"Vicki, hold up!" Becca darted around a brochure stand to catch up with the young woman before she left the building. She lowered her voice. "Can I ask… Did Molly seem okay to you? I think she was upset earlier, and I just wanted to see if her day had improved."

Tilting her head to the side, Vicki considered the question. "I wouldn't say she was upset. She has a really sharp sense of humor—sarcastic, but funny. We're going out on Thursday, because that's the next night she has off. She did get sort of quiet. Perked right up when Jace Trent came into the weight room, though. She's still there talking to him." Vicki pushed open the door, her smile impish as she turned to go. "Can't say I blame her."

Becca gritted her teeth. Although the sheriff's younger brother was closer to Molly's age than, say, Sawyer, Becca thought Jace was too old for a not-quite-nineteen-year-old.

Still, Becca had known the upstanding Trent family for years and trusted everyone in it. Jace might smile at Molly's flirting, but nothing untoward was going to happen in the heavily windowed rec-center weight room, where any number of citizens could see in. Ignoring the overprotective instinct to drag her sister out of there bodily, Becca returned to her office, her earlier triumphant mood deflated.

It wasn't a complete wash. Molly and Vicki had made plans. That counted toward establishing friendships. Of course, Vicki would be headed to Tahoe in June and back to university in August, but Molly would be more settled in by then.

Becca pushed aside thoughts of her sister long enough to answer some emails, adjust a few numbers in the summer budget and sit through a meeting with representatives from a group looking for a place to hold a haunted house in the fall. Their plans sounded too disturbing—and potentially dangerous—to host at the community center, but she agreed to a second meeting if they wanted to rethink their approach.

It was almost time to leave so Becca could pick up Marc from his after-school art program and get him to his Monday evening piano lesson. Molly was still nowhere to be seen. Jace Trent had left over an hour ago, poking his head into Becca's office to get an update on parade floats. She'd politely thanked him for his willingness to help, biting back any snarled reminders that Molly was just a kid.

Becca checked in the weight room for her sister, without luck. It would be handy to text her, but unlike many other teenagers, Molly didn't have a cell phone. She'd mentioned her ex-boyfriend giving her one, but the plan had lapsed since they broke up. Luckily, the rec center was only three stories. Becca started on the bottom floor and worked her way up, frowning when she discovered her sister in the doorway of the basketball court, smiling up at a shirtless Larry Breelan. The Breelan brothers had a reputation for trouble; the oldest, Daryl, had been arrested for fighting, public drunkenness and a number of pranks gone awry. His unapologetic "boys will be boys" attitude was particularly ludicrous now that he was approaching forty.

She cleared her throat, inserting herself between Molly and the leering Larry. "I've been looking all over the building for you," she told her sister.

"Well, you found me. Larry here was just telling me about the time he and his brothers—"

"You can tell me all about it on the way to pick up Marc. We need to go." She shot a dark look at Larry. "Now."

Molly folded her arms across her chest. "And if I'm not ready to leave? Maybe I can find my own ri—"

"You have to get ready for work tonight. Remember? Come on, I don't want Marc to think I forgot about him."

That got Molly moving. Something flashed in her expression, and Becca wondered if Odette had ever neglected to come get her once Molly's older siblings had left home. Sean and Shane had stayed in the same town, but as young bachelors enjoying their first apartment and being legally old enough to buy beer, they probably hadn't spent a lot of time in the school carpool line.

Becca gave a sigh of relief when her sister willingly followed her down the corridor. Almost as if to counteract it, Molly turned to give Larry one last wave. "Come by the Cineplex sometime."

And bring a date, Becca wanted to add. *Someone age-appropriate.*

Life would be simpler if Becca could just tell people what to do and they would listen. But politics and family matters required at least a little finesse. If she couldn't deal with her sister tactfully, how could she hope to win the election? Becca tamped down the urge to snap *what the hell were you thinking?* as they crossed the parking lot.

Instead, she silently counted to one hundred, then smiled at Molly while buckling her seat belt. "So did you have a nice afternoon? Not too boring, I hope."

FREE Merchandise is 'in the Cards' for you!

Dear Reader,

We're giving away FREE MERCHANDISE!

Seriously, we'd like to reward you for reading this novel by giving you **FREE MERCHANDISE** worth over $20 retail. And no purchase is necessary!

You see the Jack of Hearts sticker above? Paste that sticker in the box on the Free Merchandise Voucher inside. Return the Voucher today... and we'll send you Free Merchandise!

Thanks again for reading one of our novels—and enjoy your Free Merchandise with our compliments!

Pam Powers

Pam Powers

P.S. Look inside to see what Free Merchandise is **"in the cards"** for you!

W e'd like to send you two free books like the one you are enjoying now. Your two books have a combined cover price of over $10 retail, but they are yours to keep absolutely FREE! We'll even send you 2 wonderful surprise gifts. You can't lose!

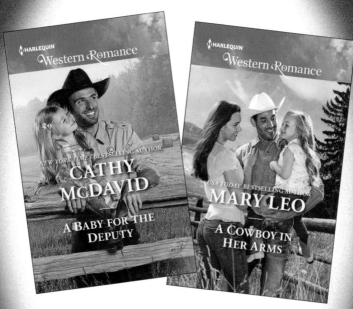

REMEMBER: Your Free Merchandise, consisting of **2 Free Books** and **2 Free Gifts**, is worth over $20 retail! No purchase is necessary, so please send for your Free Merchandise today.

Get TWO FREE GIFTS!
We'll also send you 2 wonderful FREE GIFTS (worth about $10 retail), in addition to your 2 Free books!

Visit us at:
www.ReaderService.com

YOUR FREE MERCHANDISE INCLUDES...

2 FREE Books **AND** 2 FREE Mystery Gifts

FREE MERCHANDISE VOUCHER

2 FREE
BOOKS
and
2 FREE
GIFTS

Please send my Free Merchandise, consisting of
2 Free Books and **2 Free Mystery Gifts**.
I understand that I am under no obligation to buy
anything, as explained on the back of this card.

154/354 HDL GLTC

Please Print

FIRST NAME

LAST NAME

ADDRESS

APT.#

CITY

STATE/PROV.

ZIP/POSTAL CODE

NO PURCHASE NECESSARY!

WR-517-FM17

"It was okay."

"When Vicki left the center, she mentioned the two of you might go out this week. That should be fun."

"Uh-huh."

"And Sammy—"

"Mr. Honor-Student-Captain-of-the-Swim-Team?" Molly rolled her eyes. "Did you ask him to come to the center so he could inspire your screwup sister with his rousing college pep talk?"

"Of course not! He works here. He comes in every day. And I didn't say a word to him about you beforehand. What you're calling a pep talk was just his misguided attempt to impress you."

"Right. Well, I'm sure he'll have the chance to impress plenty of girls on campus next fall."

"Look, Molly, I'm sorry if Sammy upset y—"

"I'm not upset with Sammy. *He* isn't the one who made sure I spent my afternoon with people who all have big plans and places to go. College. Lake Tahoe. Meanwhile, I'm stuck here like some loser."

Stuck? Becca's blood-pressure skyrocketed. Molly was completely ungrateful that Becca had given her a place to live and helped her find a job. *I should put her butt on a bus right back to Odette.* Sure, Becca could do that. But would she be able to live with herself afterward?

"Cupid's Bow is a wonderful place," she said firmly. "But if you don't want to be here, explore other options."

"Like school?" Molly sneered. "Did you know that Jace Trent dropped out of college?"

"Yes." His parents had been disappointed when he'd

moved back to Cupid's Bow and taken up bartending, along with several other odd jobs.

"He's been in school a lot more recently than you, and he says it's not all it's cracked up to be."

"So rather than keep an open mind about your future, you've decided to limit your options based on casual conversation with a guy you just met?" Becca was going to wring Jace's neck. *After* he finished rebuilding those floats.

Molly glared, but didn't respond. Probably just as well—they'd reached the elementary school.

Marc climbed in the car, telling them all about his day before he even had his door closed. Becca studied his freckled face in the rearview mirror, the sight of him filling her with love. She adored her son, and he would grow up knowing that.

Molly's own childhood situation had been different than Marc's. The encouragement she received was likely erratic, coming from siblings when they had time for her or Odette if she was in a rare good mood. Maybe Molly didn't dream bigger because she had trouble believing in herself. With time and patience, Becca could help her overcome that. So what if today hadn't gone perfectly? Bringing Molly to work had been a mere plan A.

And if plan A failed, there were plenty other letters in the alphabet.

"MAMA! MY LUCKY cereal isn't here!"

"Lucky cereal?" Sawyer paused in the hallway just outside the kitchen; he'd been on his way to retrieve the boots he'd left on the front porch. It was almost time to leave for Marc's soccer game.

Currently, Marc was standing in front of the open pantry, scowling fiercely. "I always have a bowl before my games. The cereal circles look like little soccer balls." He lowered his voice to a confidential tone. "And they're *chocolate*."

Ah. Sawyer guessed the kid was more invested in the splurge of almost-junk-food than he was in the athletic superstition. "Your mom took Trouble out back. Want me to look on the high shelves? Maybe the cereal just got moved."

"Hurry," Marc urged. "Or we'll run outta time."

Sawyer did his best, shuffling pantry ingredients that were so organized they were damn near shelved in alphabetical order, but there was no chocolate-flavored cereal to be found. "Sorry, buddy, I—"

"What are you guys doing?" Becca asked, as she and the puppy came in through the door from the garage. There was an undercurrent in her tone, the faint apprehension of a woman who didn't appreciate others rearranging her stuff.

"My cereal's missing," Marc explained. "Mr. Sawyer was helping me find it."

"Trying to, anyway. I'm afraid I came up short." The kid looked so crestfallen that Sawyer offered, "What if I buy you a chocolate shake after the game? We could go to the diner for supper."

Becca frowned. "Oh, I don't know about that. I—"

"Brody said the diner has awesome key lime pie." In the middle of helping his friend put out hay yesterday, Sawyer had surprised himself by asking where to find the best key lime pie in town. Sawyer's personal favorite was pecan. The request had forced him to admit that he wanted to know where to take Becca in case she ever rescinded her no-flirting policy and went out with him. It had been a random, far-fetched impulse—and yet he was glad he'd prepared. Because now her blue eyes sparkled in anticipation.

"They *do* serve good pie there," she admitted. "And it would be nice not to cook after such a long day…"

Marc let out a whoop of joy.

Becca raised an eyebrow. "I haven't technically said yes."

"But you will, right, Mama? Pretty please!"

"I suppose if you promise to show a little of that energy out on the soccer field, I can agree to the diner afterward. I have to put Trouble in her crate. Can you scoot upstairs and tell Aunt Molly we're ready to go? We need to drop her off on our way to the game."

As the boy raced out of the room, Sawyer knelt down to scratch behind the puppy's ear. "I can take care of Trouble if you need a minute to fix the pantry."

She tried hard to fake confusion, her eyes wide and her tone nonchalant. "I don't know what you mean."

"I moved some things around. I don't think all your salad dressings are in order by height anymore."

"Very funny. I'm not *that* bad." But she was already reorganizing boxes according to whatever System of Becca she used. "I'm just very busy between work and parenting and the election. It saves me time if I know where everything is. Like the cereal. It should be right here."

"I didn't touch it, I swear." He latched the metal door to Trouble's kennel. "I get in enough trouble for turning off lights when I leave a room." Go figure. He'd been brought up to believe that not wasting electricity was responsible behavior.

"Only when you turn off the ones I—"

"I'm ready," Molly announced, shrugging into her uniform vest as she entered the kitchen. "We leaving or what?"

Nodding, Becca closed the pantry door. "By any chance, did you eat Marc's cereal?"

Molly froze, her gaze turning guilty, then defensive. "I didn't see his name on the box."

"You're welcome to anything you want in the kitchen. But please, if you use something up, write it on the refrigerator list like we've talked about."

"Sorry," Molly mumbled. "I guess college-educated people never forget to do crap like that."

The sarcasm was a holdover from the day before. When Sawyer had returned from Brody's yesterday evening, the two sisters had been "discussing" regional colleges. The discussion consisted of Becca cheerfully lecturing while Molly popped bubble gum.

There was nothing cheerful in Becca's demeanor now. She balled her fists at her hips. "Are you determined to be negative about everything? My pointing out your potential was a *compliment*. Going to college—"

"A college degree isn't everything." Oh, hell. *Why did I say that?* The last thing Sawyer wanted was to get involved in the sisters' argument.

Both women swung their gazes in his direction, their matching expressions of surprise highlighting the family resemblance. Molly's shock faded to a smirk when she realized she had an ally.

Meanwhile, Becca eyed him like he was something unpleasant on the bottom of her shoe. "No," she said tightly, "of course it's not *everything*. But school is a decent starting place for a girl with academic promise and no plan."

He wouldn't know about that. Although his grades had been all right, no one had ever told him he had "academic promise." He functioned better in wide-open spaces than in classrooms. "I didn't mean—"

"You don't have to apologize to her!" Molly interjected. "People are entitled to their opinions. Even non-Becca-approved opinions. She thinks she can go through life bossing people around."

Becca's eyes narrowed dangerously. "I was *trying* to *help*. But, no, you—"

"Uh...ladies?" Though it went against his sense of self-preservation to interrupt a second time, Sawyer deemed it necessary. "Maybe this conversation should be tabled until later, so no one's late for work. Or soccer."

At the reminder of soccer, Becca whirled toward her son, paling. "Are you okay?" she asked Marc.

He looked more fascinated by the raised voices than emotionally scarred. "Fine."

"I didn't mean to lose my temper with Aunt Molly," Becca said, her tone contrite. "Sometimes adults just disagree."

Marc nodded. "I know. Mrs. W disagrees with Mr. W all the time. Kenny says his dad brings home flowers and then his parents take a nap and everything's okay."

Sawyer choked back a laugh at the mention of make-up naps.

Becca looked unsure how to respond. "Yes, well. Glad they, uh, have a system that works for them. Now, if everyone's ready, we should get going." She grabbed her car keys off the hook on the wall and strode toward the front door.

Sawyer got there first, opening the door for her. She sailed past without looking in his direction, and he wondered how badly he'd screwed up by opening his big mouth back there. He'd be happy to buy her flowers to make up for interfering, but he was pretty sure she'd never agree to a conciliatory "nap." No matter how nicely he asked.

"I'LL GET THOSE for you."

Another time, Becca might have appreciated the unsolicited offer of assistance. Now, it just made her want to slam her trunk shut—not that she could, because the automatic hydraulics kicked in, lowering the trunk with measured speed, but still. Even though it was an immature impulse, more in line with the behavior of a sulky eighteen-year-old than a pillar of the community, she didn't care. Sometimes, a woman wanted to slam something.

Or kick a very good-looking cowboy in his denim-clad shin.

Before she could tell Sawyer that she was capable of carrying the cooler and the collapsible soccer chairs she brought to every game, he was already reaching for them, taking them from her with an earnest expression.

Nice try, but it's going to take more than green-gold eyes and strong arms to win my forgiveness. No matter how great those arms looked in the short sleeves of his dark T-shirt. Who did the man think he was, butting into her conversation with Molly and undermining Becca's point? He was a guest in her home, not a family therapist. When he'd interrupted her, Becca had been so blindsided she hadn't known how to react. Too bad she didn't have that moment to do over again, she thought, as she nodded hello to team parents and the volunteer referees. Because she had a few choice words for the man.

It was unusual for her to remain this irritated— Mayor Truitt had been publicly disagreeing with her for months, and her normal response was faintly amused exasperation. So why was she so upset that Sawyer had voiced an opposing opinion? Anger was heating her blood even more than the May sun, and she impatiently pulled a rubber band from her purse, looping her hair into a ponytail. Fanning herself with her clipboard, she called the names of the kids who would play the first quarter and resolved to ignore Sawyer entirely.

But it was impossible not to notice a man on the sidelines enthusiastically yelling "Go, Unicorns!"

On some level, Becca may have been hoping that if she didn't interact much with him, then other parents wouldn't start asking questions about his association with her—a frankly ridiculous wish. Every female gaze had been drawn in Sawyer's direction from the second he put down the cooler, some admiring, but most of them quizzical. As the second quarter started, it became clear Sawyer was specifically cheering for her son. He clapped for the team in general, but Marc was the only kid whose name he knew. The quizzical glances shifted from Sawyer to Becca. As she swapped out a couple players, she struggled to ignore the unspoken questions shimmering around her like heat waves.

But what she *couldn't* ignore was the giddy expression on her son's face. Marc had never looked this happy playing soccer. Ever. And she knew she had Sawyer to thank for that.

Just moments before the halftime whistle, Marc kicked in a goal. Pride crashed through Becca, and she barely checked the urge to rush over and hug her kid. He might not appreciate that in front of all these people, and, as coach, she should treat her players equally. So she clapped him on the shoulder and said "Good job" just as she would have congratulated Doug or Jodie. But inside, she was turning cartwheels. *I knew you could do it, champ.*

When the players cleared the field for their halftime break, Sawyer helped distribute water and orange slices from the cooler. Behind her, Becca heard Mrs. Prescott asking him, "Are you Marc's uncle?"

"No, ma'am. I'm just renting an apartment from the Johnstons until after the centennial celebration."

"Oh." Cecily White, the single mother of twins, sighed audibly. "It's a shame you can't stay longer. You seem to be bringing our team good luck."

"I appreciate that," Sawyer said, "but I suspect the team is doing well thanks to its stellar coach."

Becca's cheeks tingled with warmth. *Charmer.* Did he know she could hear him? Did he really think she was doing a "stellar" job, or was this another attempt to get back in her good graces?

A moment later, Cecily elbowed Becca in the ribs, whispering, "I can't believe you've been hiding him up in your attic!"

Hiding implied keeping secrets—a less than ideal reputation for a political candidate. "He's a tenant," Becca said coolly, "not a hostage. Free to come and go as he pleases."

Cecily hadn't heard a word. She was too busy ogling Sawyer as he high-fived the smallest player on the team. "You are a lucky, lucky woman."

Becca almost laughed at that. While she certainly had her share of blessings—namely her son and the friends she'd made in this town—*lucky* did not describe how she'd been feeling lately.

"I was so sad for you when Colin left," Cecily continued, "but if I'd known *he* was going to come riding into your life…"

Yeah, well. Pretty soon, he'd be riding right back out of it. "Cecily, if you don't mind, I want to talk to the kids about their passing strategy before we start again." She also needed to remind them that the teams switched goals after halftime. Many was the game when Dylan Ellis got so excited to find himself in control of the ball that he kicked to whichever net was closest and scored a point for the other team.

She gathered the kids around her, but while she was waiting for the last stragglers to join the semicircle, Amy Prescott sidled up to her.

"Kudos on your new cowboy friend," Amy said. "I don't know where you find the time—or the energy— with everything else you've got going on, but—"

"Amy. Sawyer is renting a room from me. Period. It doesn't take much extra time or effort to deposit his rent check."

Amy winked broadly. "Hey, no judgment here. You're my hero."

Becca ground her molars, turning her attention to the antsy seven-year-olds, who were turning out to be far less frustrating than their parents.

To Sawyer's credit, his behavior throughout the entire game was impeccable. He was friendly but not flirty with the moms, overlooking their obvious titters and speculation. He cheered heartily for the Unicorns but politely clapped when the other team did well, underscoring all Becca's lectures about sportsmanship. And not once did he crowd her or monopolize her time, instead hanging back and letting her coach.

Yet she could feel his gaze on her so often, like the prickly warning of sunburn. She'd slathered both herself and Marc with UV protection; too bad they didn't make a Sawyer-block that would keep her from getting emotionally burned. She'd had time for her anger to cool, and now realized that while she'd been annoyed that he jumped into her conversation with Molly and contradicted the point Becca was trying to make, what she'd really been feeling was hurt. Betrayed, even. It was an overreaction that underscored how important Sawyer's opinion was becoming—how important *he* was becoming—to her.

She could tell anyone who would listen that he was nothing more than a tenant, but if that were true, he wouldn't have the power to hurt her feelings. From the first time she'd laid eyes on him, there had been attraction. Now there were stirrings of emotion that wouldn't do either of them any good in the long run. *And I always think long-term.* Becca had goals and plans and a track record of success…except when it came to men.

After two and a half years together, her high school sweetheart had accused her of caring more about her potential scholarships than she did about him; their relationship dissolved when she told him he was absolutely right. In college, she'd met her husband-to-be, and he had seemed like her fairy-tale prince, everything she'd ever dreamed of in the man she would someday marry. Then she'd come with him to Cupid's Bow and got her happily-ever-after. Sort of.

The truth was, even though she was a mother past thirty, she didn't have a lot of experience with men. She could count on her fingers the number of guys she'd dated. She wasn't used to flirting or casual relationships, and now that she was divorced, she sure as hell wasn't looking for Fairytale Prince: The Sequel. So she was unsure how to handle Sawyer. Could she go on a few dates with someone and enjoy the pleasure of his company, knowing that there was no future in it, or would it feel like a counterproductive waste of her limited time?

Next to her, Amy Prescott shouted, startling Becca from her thoughts. Jodie had scored. *My team got a point and I was too distracted by a man to even notice.* Some coach she was.

Becca belatedly cheered on her star player, working hard to stay focused on the game for the last few plays. But once the final whistle blew and Sawyer helped her gather gear, she felt uncharacteristically shy, self-conscious in a way she hadn't experienced since her dramatic growth spurt in elementary school.

"Thanks," she mumbled as he handed her the clipboard. "Not just for helping me carry stuff or pass out snacks, but for being here. It meant a lot to Marc." The Fighting Frogs had defeated the Unicorns 7–5, but from the way her son was beaming, no one would ever guess his team had lost. Marc had scored two goals, a season record for him, and both times he'd turned immediately to Sawyer to exchange a thumbs-up. Now Marc was jogging toward them with a rare swagger.

She ruffled her son's hair. "You more than earned that milk shake. There may even be onion rings in your future. Great job, champ."

"Thanks, Mama. What did you think, Mr. Sawyer? Was that great? What was your favorite part? I liked scoring goals, but also that time when the other team thought I would pass to Jodie but actually I kicked it to Doug, and they didn't even see him coming! And when Dylan wiped out, making that totally awesome kick— it's okay, he said he's not hurt—and…" Marc kept up a mile-a-minute sports commentary as the three of them walked to the minivan.

Listening to his high-energy recap made Becca realize how much her own energy was flagging. After a full day's work, the argument with her sister and the game, she was beat. Although she'd never say a word to dampen Marc's enthusiasm for their trip to the diner, what she really wanted was to go home to a hot shower, silky-soft pajamas and a good book. Sighing, she hit the remote that unlocked the van doors. *I'd be willing to forgo key lime pie for the chance to kick off my shoes and take off this bra.*

"You okay?" Sawyer asked.

"Of course. It's just been a long day."

"Want me to drive?" he asked. "I've been tooling around town enough that I can find my way to Main Street from here."

Her instinctive reaction was to refuse; she believed in projecting an image of strength. But, honestly, being able to close her eyes in the passenger seat for a few minutes sounded like heaven. "Here." She gave him the keys, her hand brushing his.

His warm, callused fingers against hers sent a pulse

of awareness through her, but the brief physical contact wasn't nearly as intimate as his reaction. He went still at her touch, his only movement a shuddery breath as his eyes locked with hers. She might not have abundant experience with the opposite sex, but there was no mistaking the desire she saw in his gaze. It made her feel wanted and feminine. And powerful.

Her earlier fatigue evaporated as if it had never been. Once again, key lime pie sounded like a splendid idea—or at least like a safe substitute for what she was really craving.

SEATED NEXT TO her on the padded vinyl bench, Marc was buzzing with so much excitement that the salt and pepper shakers on the table were living up to their name.

And I ordered this kid a chocolate milk shake? Becca was having serious second thoughts about filling him up with sugar. On the plus side, after the crash, maybe he'd go to bed early. Yeah, there was some A-plus parenting.

While Becca perused the salad choices, Marc leaned across the table. "Do you know what you want, Mr. Sawyer?"

Sawyer's eyes were on Becca, his menu unopened in front of him. "Yes."

Heat flooded her cheeks, and she glanced away, trying not to project her own lust onto the cowboy. She noticed the Ruiz family at a corner table; she was fairly certain their little boy had been in Marc's class last year. "Hey, Marc, isn't that one of your friends?"

Marc spun around, climbing up on his knees for a better look. "Uh-huh. That's Alejandro. He sits at the same art table as me on Fridays. He's a real good draw-er."

"Do you want to go say hi?" she asked. "We have plenty of time." His milk shake would be out soon, but they hadn't ordered their food yet. It would be at least another ten minutes before dinner was served.

"Okay." He scrambled down and darted into the path of an oncoming waitress. Luckily, she had the reflexes of a superhero and didn't spill any of the drinks she carried.

"Walking feet!" Becca called after her son. Then she turned to Sawyer with a wry smile. "Is it wrong that I desperately want him to become better friends with someone who doesn't own a snake?" She fiddled with the straw in her sweet tea. "No, in all seriousness, I'm incredibly grateful he's got a best friend who's helped him get through some tough transitions. But I worry that because of my schedule he's spending too much time with the Whittmeyers."

Sawyer cocked his head, his expression puzzled. "Whittmeyer... Whittmeyer... Gee, the name doesn't ring a bell."

That made her laugh. "If I had a dollar for every time I heard a story that started with 'Kenny Whittmeyer,' I'd be the richest woman in Texas." She glanced fondly at her son. From his exuberant body language, she guessed he was reenacting the soccer game for his friend, especially the parts where Marc scored goals. "I know I told you this already, but thank you for coming to the game."

"I had fun," Sawyer said, sounding vaguely surprised. "And now there's something I should have told you already. I'm sorry about what happened at the house, with your sister. No one asked for my input, and I should have kept my trap shut. College is…a sore spot for me."

"Because you didn't go?" she asked carefully. Though she hadn't admitted it to him, she'd looked up some of his articles online. His intelligent, evocative writing had impressed her. He was descriptive enough to bring to life sights and sounds and tastes of places she'd never been, witty enough that she'd laughed aloud at her computer screen. And when referencing a historic massacre that was an uglier part of the state's history, and how people could learn from it, his words had been poignant enough to make her blink away tears. He was definitely as smart as any of the college friends who'd graduated alongside her.

"I didn't mind not going," he said. "I was being honest when I told Molly that I don't think a college degree is the be-all and end-all. People take different paths in life. But when my brother came home from college…"

Had Sawyer resented his brother's education? Had he felt somehow inferior? It was impossible to imagine the cocky cowboy ever feeling not good enough. "What did—"

The waitress returned to the table with Marc's milk shake and an apology for taking so long. "I've got a party of twelve over there, including two dairy allergies and a gluten allergy." She nodded to the other side of the room, where tables had been pushed together to accommodate half a dozen kids in soccer jerseys and their parents. The Unicorns were only one of the teams who'd recently finished a game. "Checking with the chef on substitutions and ingredients got hectic."

Becca assured her that the wait was no problem.

Truthfully, she'd been so caught up in wanting to learn more about Sawyer's past that she'd forgotten about food entirely. But her son certainly hadn't. As if he'd been keeping one eye on the table for the arrival of his milk shake, he materialized immediately, wriggling back into the booth with a huge smile and a request to take Trouble for a walk in the park sometime with Alejandro's dog, Scottie.

Guiltily, Becca realized that she was a little disappointed that Marc had returned so soon, curtailing her grown-up conversation with Sawyer. *It would be nice to have dinner alone with him.* The thought triggered an unsettling realization. Although she'd told Sawyer he shouldn't flirt with her, shouldn't ask her out, if he did…she would say yes.

She took a deep breath, not sure whether to hope he honored her request or to hope he was stubborn enough to ask anyway.

Chapter Nine

"This is *not* me giving in to your 5:00 a.m. howls," Becca told the puppy sternly. "Because that would be reinforcing negative behavior. This is just me taking you outside to further your house-training, since we're both awake, anyway."

Trouble didn't seem to care what the reasoning was. She bolted forward with her customary enthusiasm the minute Becca unlatched the kennel. Since Becca had sleepily stumbled into the master bathroom, where the dog was, it seemed inconsiderate not to also give the shepherd the chance to go potty. She carried the puppy downstairs, where the leash hung on a newly installed hook, and as she did so, the most delicious aroma in the world washed over her. *Coffee.*

Maybe that had been what woke her, not the puppy's intermittent whimpering. *Truth time, Rebecca—did you come down here to walk the puppy or to say good-bye to Sawyer before he hits the road?* Well, it wasn't as if the two were mutually exclusive.

Refugio was only a couple hours from here; she was stunned that someone would voluntarily make a trip this early. But Sawyer said he was stopping at a ranch along the way to have breakfast and check on some business investments. It sounded as if he had friends in the area that he wanted to visit, too. Like Brody, here in Cupid's Bow. Thinking of Kate and Sierra and Hadley, Becca wondered what it would be like if her friends were scattered throughout the state. She couldn't decide if Sawyer was blessedly popular, with so many people in his life, or lonely. Maybe those conditions weren't mutually exclusive, either.

As she padded into the kitchen, she wondered... Did Sawyer also have lovers all over the state, women he called when he was in town who would be happy to see him?

Her tone was sharper than she'd intended when she greeted him with, "You turned on the wrong light. Again." She had one programmed; it helped give the house the appearance of being occupied when she was away and insured that she didn't come downstairs to total darkness on early mornings. When he used the switch manually, he disrupted the timer.

"Good morning to you, too."

"Sorry. The puppy's been interrupting my sleep." She had no qualms about blaming her mood on the squirming bundle of fur in her arms. At the shepherd's insistent wiggling, she set Trouble down, freeing her to run to Sawyer with floppy-pawed adoration. Trouble's feet were comically big for her body, but she didn't let awkwardness stop her from throwing herself atop Sawyer's boots for a tummy rub. The dog obviously loved him—and why not? He had rescued her from a storm and given her a home. Yet after a moment's affection, she loyally returned to Becca.

He grinned. "She knows who the alpha of the pack is." *Now if only the* rest *of the pack would recognize my authority.* As she took the puppy into the backyard, Becca thought irritably about Sawyer disrupting her light settings, and Molly finishing the oranges in the produce drawer and the milk *and* the last of Marc's cereal without writing any of it down on the grocery memo pad. Did no one respect Becca's carefully ordered world, the effort she put into keeping life's chaos at bay? *Don't panic.* It was only some lightbulbs and supermarket items. That didn't mean she was losing control. Yet.

She went back inside, hoping caffeine would improve her outlook. Sawyer leaned against the kitchen counter, watching her pour a cup of coffee.

He slid her the sugar canister. "Not going back to sleep?"

"No point. I have to be up in less than an hour to get Marc ready for school, anyway." All year, her son fought getting out of bed. It was ironic that only in the final two weeks of school, excited by the promise of summer, did he wake alert and cooperative. "Besides, I have a grudging respect for this time of day. I don't like it, exactly, but I appreciate the peace of it." They were speaking in hushed tones, careful not to wake the rest of the household. Outside was hushed, too. At 5:00 a.m., the world was just waking up and the chaos hadn't kicked in.

She stirred her coffee. "What about you? Natural morning person?"

"Not inherently, no. But after so many years of my dad waking me for early morning chores, the habit sank in. It helps when I wake up to a pretty lady, but as long as there's coffee, I can cope."

She ignored the pretty-lady crack; she doubted a

woman with tangled hair and light-timer issues qualified. They finished their coffee in companionable silence.

Rinsing his mug out at the sink, he gave her a crooked smile. "Will you miss me while I'm gone?"

She rolled her eyes. "If you want me to miss you, you have to stay away for more than one day."

"Can't. Your cooking's got me too spoiled."

Another eye roll. Conversations with Sawyer were like ocular calisthenics. "I get it—you're an irredeemable charmer who can't help laying it on thick. But, come on. Respect my intelligence, would you? In the week you've been here, we've had pizza, deli takeout, diner food and hamburgers *you* grilled." In fact, now that she recounted the list aloud, she felt vaguely embarrassed. She actually was a fair cook, but she'd been so busy lately...

"You're right, commenting on the food was an inferior use of my charm. I can do better." He cleared his throat, his expression faux solemn. "Rodeos are dangerous work, ma'am. I'd be much obliged if you'd send me off with a kiss for good luck."

For one ludicrous second, she imagined actually doing it, going up on her toes and pressing her lips to his just to see his shocked expression. It would be priceless. *And that would be your* only *motivation?* Well, no. There was also the rediscovery of what it would be like to kiss a man—to kiss this man, in particular. *Bad idea, Becca.* Yet her heart sped up, and anticipation fizzed through her. Gripping her coffee mug, she stood rooted to the spot. Her common sense was strong enough to overcome anticipation. For now.

Sawyer grinned, and the reckless moment passed

with him none the wiser. "Okay, that line was terrible, too. I can't do my best work at this hour."

"You're not supposed to be flirting with me, anyway, remember?"

"Of course." His expression was all innocence. "That was only hypothetical flirting. It didn't count. And I still get to be *friendly*…that's just good manners."

How long would her self-discipline hold? She grabbed his truck keys from the counter and held them out. "You should go. Now, before morning traffic picks up. Be a damn shame if you got stuck in Cupid's Bow rush hour." All nine cars and two school buses of it.

He laughed, taking his keys and tipping his hat in farewell. Beyond the kitchen, too far in the shadows of the hallway for her to see his face, he paused for just a second. "Now that I think about it, maybe it isn't the food here I like so much. Maybe it's just seeing you across the table."

"You were incredible!"

Any man would appreciate hearing that from a pretty woman, and Sawyer smiled at the willowy brunette in her halter top and skintight jeans. But most of his attention was on the chute, where one of his best friends was about to ride. Lewis had been injured last winter, and this was his first official event back in the saddle.

"Thanks, darlin'," Sawyer said absently. He'd sound ungracious if he disputed her compliment, but today hadn't been one of his better performances. *Because you weren't focused enough.*

He'd been distracted and out of sorts. His morning had started off so well, teasing Becca in the cozy confines of her kitchen. Good coffee, better company. But when he'd reached the ranch where his friend and business partner, Kaleb, lived, he'd felt a pang of… Not quite bitterness, but perhaps an envy that men like Brody and Kaleb had a place where they belonged.

How long had it been since Sawyer felt that? Maybe it was why he'd been so angry at Charlie—not just for coming back from college with a condescending disrespect for the work Sawyer had done in his absence, but for making Sawyer feel like the ranch wasn't equally his, like he belonged less.

Although Sawyer still enjoyed traveling, discovering quirky new places and regional customs to write about, the word *home* was starting to hold an allure he hadn't experienced since he'd driven away from his family ranch with a muttered good riddance.

Only distantly registering that his brunette fan had faded back into the crowd, he cheered for Lewis, eager to replace the ugly memory of his friend's accident. *You're lucky* you *didn't have an accident today.* Bronc riding was not something that should be half-assed. What had happened to the thrill of the ride?

Sawyer used to love the crowds and the noise; always happiest outdoors, he hadn't minded the gritty heat. Even the sensation of his teeth rattling in his skull had made him feel alive, sending jolts of adrenaline through him. He knew cowboys who participated in rodeos well into their sixties, albeit on the senior circuit, but when Sawyer thought about the decades to come, this wasn't what he wanted for his future. At least, it wasn't *all* he wanted.

But the packed stand of a Texas rodeo was no place

for introspection. Someone jostled his shoulder, and he turned to find Gabe Delgado, champion roper, standing there.

"Been a long time." Gabe winced in mock sympathy. "Sorry to see you've gotten even uglier since I saw you last."

"You haven't—but then it's hard to go down when you were already at rock bottom."

Gabe cackled at that. "Did Lewis talk to you about tonight? A bunch of us are going to The Catfish Shack. Knock back a few cervezas, charm some pretty senoritas… You in?"

"Absolutely." For the beer, anyway. Sawyer's interest in flirting with attractive women was as halfhearted as his lamentable ride. *Not true.* He recalled the way Becca had looked this morning, when she'd grinned at him and sassed that he needed to get out of her house before rush hour. As tired and dusty as he was, he knew that if *she* were at the restaurant tonight, where scheduled bands performed everything from zydeco music to Czech polkas, his interest would be boundless. He'd want to take her out on the dance floor…and back to his hotel room.

With the festival kicking off this weekend, there would be numerous events where he could indulge his first wish; maybe she would agree to dance with him. As for his second wish? *Ha.* Yet it felt as if the magnetic pull between them had been steadily growing. Was there a chance Becca had changed her mind?

Sawyer grinned, already looking forward to seeing her tomorrow. The thrill of rodeo riding might be starting to fade, but there were plenty of other challenges that could keep his life exciting.

GOOD TO BE BACK HOME. The uncensored thought jolted Sawyer worse than the potholes that had threatened his tire rims and shocks just outside the county line. He turned off the truck, staring through the windshield at Becca's place. This was no more "home" than any of the circuit hotels he'd stayed in or bunkhouses he'd shared with other ranch hands when he picked up seasonal work. And yet it felt more welcoming than the tiny apartment he rented as his base of operations, probably because he was never there long enough to settle in or decorate beyond the essentials—a bed and a TV.

Never mind the "home" part, he told himself as he rounded the house to the back stairs and his private entrance. *It's just nice to be back where there's a generous-sized tub.* He'd awakened this morning with some predictably sore muscles and a few new bruises. Some mineral salt and a soak in that claw-foot tub sounded like heaven. After the nonstop activity of the rodeo yesterday and last night's rollicking good time at the noisy club, he was looking forward to the peace and quiet, too. He doubted anyone would be home midmorning on a Thursday. Marc should be in school, Becca was probably at work and Molly... No telling, but he was sure Becca had her somewhere—applying for a receptionist job, volunteering at the local food bank, taking an aptitude test.

He didn't doubt that Becca's intentions were good, but did she realize that her manic efforts could backfire? Molly might resent being pressed into service 24/7 and rebel. What if she got herself fired from the theater or tanked a community college application just to give herself a break?

None of my business, though. He'd interfered once and regretted it. From here on out, the Baker sisters would have to work out their own differences of opinion.

Still…seeing their sibling relationship with the clarity of an outsider's perspective was making him think more about his own brother. They'd been so close once; part of him missed that. Maybe he'd give Charlie a call some night soon. He still hadn't congratulated him in person about the baby—not that over the phone was in person, exactly, but it was better than a text.

As expected, the house was empty.

But not entirely quiet. He'd just removed his shirt and pulled the mineral salt from the cabinet under the bathroom sink when he heard Trouble barking furiously. Obviously, she'd heard him moving around upstairs. She'd probably been in her crate for hours; taking her outside before he indulged in his bath was the humane thing to do.

He had to pass through Becca's room to reach the master bath where the kennel was, and being in her private sanctuary felt odd. The room was so intensely *female*…from faint lingering perfume in the air to the pale pink curtains and the jewelry box on her dresser. Her bed almost made him laugh; it was made with military precision. Although he'd never do it, his fingers itched to scoot one of the decorative throw pillows a millimeter to the side, as an experiment to see whether Becca would notice. *Of course she would. Then she'd rightfully toss you out into the street for touching her personal things.*

No more fixating on her bed. Or the idea of her in it. Or the pleasant fantasy of sharing it with her. He groaned. At this rate, he should skip the muscle-healing bath and take a cold shower instead.

From the bathroom came a yip of impatience, and he gave himself an inner shake. Right. Dog, bath, move on with his day. As he unlatched the kennel, Trouble tripped over her own feet, scrabbling to reach him and lick his face.

"Could we turn the adoration down to, like, a nine?" he asked, holding her at arm's length. "I like you, but no doggy kisses."

Growing up, he'd talked to the pintos and Arabian horses in the barn, so he didn't feel self-conscious about his one-sided conversation with Trouble. At least, he didn't until he heard Becca advise from the bedroom beyond, "Maybe you should start with holding paws and work your way up to kisses."

A dozen reactions hit at once—from being embarrassed to hoping she wasn't angry at his intrusion to being plain old happy to hear her voice—and he lost his grip on the puppy. Trouble bounded over to meet her mistress. Sawyer rose slowly, following at a more dignified speed. "Hope I wasn't overstepping in here," he called. "I just got in and thought Trouble could use..." He caught sight of her for the first time and her expression robbed him of words. She was gaping at him with raw appreciation that made his pulse quicken. He didn't know what he'd been about to say; he only knew that if she kept looking at him like that, his jeans were going to get seriously uncomfortable.

She swallowed. "You, ah... Your shirt."

He'd forgotten he was only half-dressed; it hadn't seemed important when he'd had the house to himself. "Sorry?" He couldn't commit to the word. While he hoped he hadn't offended her, he couldn't regret the way her gaze greedily traveled over him. "I thought you were at work."

She nodded, her voice huskier than usual. "I was. The school called—Marc forgot his lunch, so I was going to grab it and drop it off. But I figured I should let Trouble out while I was here…"

"Great minds think alike," he teased, stopping in front of her. But neither of them was actually moving to let the dog outside. Instead, they stood still, only inches apart, and Sawyer wondered if kissing her would be the smartest or dumbest thing he'd ever done. Damn, he wanted it, to feel her mouth beneath his, but she'd warned him off and he wasn't going to push without a clear signal from her that she wanted it, too. So he balled his hands into fists to keep from reaching for her, and willed her to do something crazy—like pull him down on that perfectly made bed and have her wicked way with him.

When Trouble barked, breaking the moment and stealing Becca's attention, he felt a flare of irrational resentment toward the dog. *I snagged you a home, and this is how you repay me? Thanks a lot, mutt.*

Becca scooped up the puppy. "I better get her outside before there are consequences."

"Probably a wise choice." To his own ears, his voice sounded thick with disappointment. Did she notice? It was difficult to tell, since she was speed-walking in the opposite direction.

Sawyer followed her to the kitchen, where she was hooking the leash to Trouble's collar. "I'll take her out. You have to get back to work and swing by the school, so…"

"And you have writing to do?" she asked, as he opened the door.

Right. Travel articles about the great state of Texas and places where the cowboy way of life still persisted. He'd only ever written nonfiction, yet he suddenly felt inspired to try his hand at erotic short stories.

"They're good," Becca said sincerely.

Blinking, he whirled around to face her. She enjoyed erotic short stories?

"Your pieces, I mean."

"Oh." Reason belatedly caught up to his brain. But then he felt confused again. "You've read them?"

Her smile bordered on shy. "A few. They made me realize that even though I've lived in Texas all my life, there are a lot of places I've never visited, landmarks I'd love to see. New experiences I'd like to try."

Be glad to help with that, sweetheart. "I'm glad they had an effect on you. That's gratifying to hear."

Marc's lunch box in hand, she followed him outside, choosing to go around the house to her minivan instead of through the front door. "Then I'm glad I told you. I was…a little embarrassed to admit it."

"Embarrassed you read a couple of nonfiction articles written in the specific hopes people would read them? Why?"

"Embarrassed to be looking you up on the computer when I was supposed to be working. Or after I crawled into bed at night. It was a surreal experience, reading the words of a man who happened to be sleeping one floor above me."

She'd been in bed thinking about him. Without the tail of a shirt to help camouflage his growing erection, he turned away, letting Trouble explore some bushes in the opposite direction.

After a moment, Becca said, "I'd better scoot. Have a good afternoon."

"You, too." He tried to sound casual and not like a man choking on his own lust. "I'll see you tonight." And no doubt be thinking of her in all the hours in between.

BECCA STIRRED THE peppered white gravy that had once won a Cupid's Bow cook-off; it was funny to think about how hard she'd worked to impress the judges when she first moved here and realize that next week *she* would be one of the judges. Also, now that she thought about it, it might be a little funny that they even had a gravy cook-off. Did other places do that? Maybe it was a small-town Texas thing; the quality of one's chicken-fried steak was determined largely by the gravy that went over it.

And tonight she was making her from-scratch chicken-fried steak, gravy and mashed potatoes. Normally, she coached soccer practice Thursday evenings, but since they were under a storm warning and the kids had just played two nights ago, she'd exercised her coach's prerogative and canceled. For the first time since Sawyer had moved in, she was demonstrating her real cooking skills. Hopefully, it would impress him—because she was psyching herself up to ask him out.

She could no longer deny what she wanted. Those few moments when he'd been shirtless in her bedroom today? Hotter than the last few times she'd actually been in bed with her ex-husband.

Only a few days ago, she'd told Molly that she was

someone who seized opportunity. And, with soccer practice out of the way, tonight was a unique opportunity. Molly and Vicki had headed into town for an evening at the local dance hall, and once Marc went to take his shower, Becca and Sawyer would have a few minutes of privacy. She could ask him to the concert Sunday. Or they could make reservations for the nice restaurant over in Turtle. Even the idea of opening some wine and watching the storm after Marc went to bed sounded like a promising date. Since Vicki would be bringing Molly home after their girls' night, Becca had nowhere she had to be.

Last night, when Sawyer had been away, she'd spent a lot of time thinking about him, thinking about how he'd be gone for real soon. And she'd come to realize that if they didn't have at least one date before he left, she'd regret it. It had been a lonely two years since her divorce, and she might be in for quite a few more. Meanwhile, fate had delivered to her doorstep a funny, articulate, dead-sexy cowboy whose abs could have been sculpted from marble. Who was she to ignore that gift?

The fact that he was so good with her kid was also heart melting. He was outside with Marc now, helping him pick flowers to press for science class.

When the door banged shut and the two of them came in, Trouble on their heels, Becca admonished her son to wash his hands extra carefully before dinner.

"Good idea," Sawyer said. "I'm going to my room to wash up, too." He was back a few minutes later in a fresh T-shirt, holding his hands out toward Becca. "I used soap and everything," he teased. His playful expression faded as he inhaled deeply. "Lord, it smells good in here. Amazing, actually."

"Let's hope the food tastes that way, too," she said lightly. She wasn't worried. Well, not about the dinner, anyway. Thinking ahead to later gave her butterflies. *Get a grip. You are not afraid to make the first move.*

But maybe the butterflies weren't a sign of fear. Maybe the fluttering was just giddy expectation. Now that she'd stopped trying to fight her attraction to him, it was stronger than ever. Each glance in his direction left her a little breathless, quivery with awareness and suppressed need. She wouldn't have been surprised if she dropped a plate while trying to set the table.

Marc returned, and once he'd presented his hands for inspection, they all sat down to eat. After his first bite of food, Sawyer gave a low moan, his expression one of rapture.

"You can cook like *this*, yet you still order pizzas?" he demanded.

She grinned, pleased by the compliment. "Well, this is pretty time-consuming. If it weren't for practice being rained out…" She cast a guilty look at the sunshine streaming through the kitchen window. The weather front that had originally been forecast for this evening had veered south of them. "Anyway, I love to do it when I get the rare opportunity, but life doesn't always cooperate. So eat up. Tomorrow we're probably back to hot dogs or frozen lasagna."

Marc scrunched his nose. "Why would anyone eat lasagna that's frozen? Blecch."

"No, I'd cook it in the oven first."

"Then it wouldn't be frozen," he pointed out with exaggerated patience. "You're weird, Mama."

Sawyer winked at her from across the table. "But good weird."

MOST DAYS, BECCA would give just about anything to slow down time—so that she could have more hours to spend with her son, more hours to research the feasibility of plans for the town, more hours to exercise and work off all that key lime pie. Yet tonight was moving so slowly that she wanted to scream in frustration. Dinner had been wonderful; if the way to a man's heart was really through his stomach, Sawyer would be proposing any minute now.

But as soon as they were done eating, while Becca struggled to find a reason to send Marc up to shower an hour early, her son tugged Sawyer into the other room so they could finish watching an eighties' sci-fi movie they'd started before Sawyer had gone on his overnight trip. Marc had been waiting days to see the end. So while the guys laughed through a movie with terrible special effects and no discernible plot line, she cleaned the kitchen. Thoroughly. She had a lot of excess energy tonight, and while scrubbing counters and appliances wasn't her first choice for burning through it, chicken-fried steak *was* a messy meal to prepare. Might as well put her vigor to good use.

When she heard the music of the end credits, excitement tingled through her. There was a definite spring in her step as she moved to the doorway of the living room. "Marc, honey, why don't you head up and take your shower now? Or…"

Inspiration struck. "Would you rather take a bath? You still have that art kit Ms. Hadley gave you for your birthday." It included colored bubbles and special crayons that could be used on the tile and generally made a mess—which Marc loved but she did not. Tonight, she would be willing for him to linger a bit longer in the tub while he colored and played. *I am a very selfish mom.*

He grinned eagerly. "Cool! Can I get my toy boats and my water gun, too?"

She was going to be mopping up puddles from the floor afterward. "Sure."

Sawyer chuckled as he rose from the sofa. "I think I've been doing baths wrong. I had one earlier today, but it lacked art supplies and a fleet of ships."

Becca smiled over her son's head and almost joked that now she knew what to get Sawyer as a parting gift, but the idea of saying goodbye to him made something inside her clench. Instead she told Sawyer, "I'm going to run upstairs and help Marc start his bath." If she didn't supervise the pouring of bubbles, the entire second floor would be suds city. "But after that, I, uh, I was hoping you and I could talk."

His eyebrows rose. "Did I forget to write something on the grocery pad?"

"It's nothing like that."

"Well, you have my interest piqued. How about I take Trouble for a quick walk, you take care of Marc and we'll meet back here in about ten minutes?"

Her heart raced. "Deal."

Chapter Ten

Don't jump to conclusions, don't jump to conclusions.
It had been Sawyer's mantra all the way up the street.
Just because Becca wanted some time alone with him
didn't guarantee that she wanted to further explore the
chemistry that had sizzled between them earlier today.
Still, with that impressive homemade dinner and the
way she'd smiled when they agreed to meet back in a
few minutes, it was difficult not to get his hopes up.

"Hello, Sawyer!" Elderly Mrs. Spiegel was playing
chess with her husband on the front porch, and they
both waved in his direction. Earlier in the week, Sawyer had helped Mrs. Spiegel get her car started after
her battery died. He'd heard from Brody—who'd heard
from his aunt Marie—that Mrs. Spiegel was telling everyone in town that Sawyer was a hero.

He waved back at the Spiegels, trying to look like
a respectable citizen and not a pervert who wanted
to get naked with his landlady at the soonest opportunity. *You may have misread the signals.* But just in
case, he quickened his steps, urging Trouble back to
the house. When he took the leash into the kitchen to
hang on its appropriate hook, he found Becca pouring
two glasses of wine.

She peered up at him from beneath her lashes. "I hope you like red."

Truthfully, he was more of a beer guy, but with any luck, this was a special occasion. "Red is perfect."

"I have a confession to make," she said. "You remember when I told you that you'd have to be gone for more than a night for me to miss you?"

He nodded.

"I lied. Turns out I did miss you last night. Does that sound ridiculous?"

"Not even a little." Should he admit that the whole time he was out with his buddies, surrounded by pretty women, he couldn't get her off his mind? "I—"

The phone rang, and Becca swore. He almost laughed; her uncharacteristic cursing perfectly matched how he felt about the interruption.

Leaning over to glance at the caller ID, she frowned. "It's the deputy. Probably just festival red tape, but I'd better take it."

"I'm not going anywhere." Now that he was sure they were both feeling the same way, he was suddenly calmer, more centered. He didn't have to wonder *what if* anymore; he could afford to be patient for the space of a phone call.

She gave his hand a brief, grateful squeeze, then picked up the cordless receiver. "Hello?" A second later, she paled.

"What is it?" Sawyer blurted. He hadn't meant to interrupt, but worry for her eclipsed courtesy.

She barely seemed to hear him, anyway. Wearing a dazed, shell-shocked expression that was very un-Becca, she nodded into the phone. "I... Yes, thank you. I'll be right there."

As soon as she hung up, he stepped closer, folding her in a loose hug. Despite the erotic thoughts he'd had about her, he didn't have any ulterior motives for holding her now; he was simply driven by the need to comfort. "Everything okay?" *Dumb ass. Police officers don't call at night for no reason.*

"Fine." She expelled a shaky breath. "Except for my underage sister being loudly drunk and kicked out of the dance hall."

He winced. Molly certainly wasn't the first teenager in the world to have a couple drinks—Sawyer was relieved the news hadn't been worse—but this must be a blow to Becca. She'd been working hard to shape her sister into a model citizen; he wouldn't be surprised if Becca saw this as a failure on her part.

She moved her glass of wine away, suddenly eyeing the alcohol as if it was corrosive acid. "I need to go get her."

"Want me to come with you?" The offer was automatic. As much as he hated family drama, it turned out that he hated seeing her upset even more. He desperately wanted to make this better for her.

A half-formed smile ghosted across her lips. "That's sweet, but no. Can you stay with Marc while I run out?"

"Of course. And Becca?" He gave her his most solemn expression. "I promise not to adopt any more pets while you're gone."

She laughed then, a peal of pure amusement, and in that moment, he felt every bit the hero Mrs. Spiegel said he was.

WHEN BECCA ROLLED into the gravel parking lot, she spotted her sister immediately. It was difficult to miss

Molly, who was gesticulating wildly next to a police car parked in the corner. Becca squinted, studying the scene in the dim orange glow of sporadic light poles. Molly looked furious even though she was at fault, not at all grateful that Deputy Thomas had called her sister instead of hauling her to the station.

On the rare occasions Becca had overimbibed, she tended to become chatty, giggly or weepy. *The lesser-known dwarves.* It occurred to her for the first time since the deputy's call that Molly might be an angry drunk. While Becca couldn't bring herself to believe her sister would turn violent or ever hurt Marc, she had no trouble imagining Molly dropping f-bombs from one end of the house to the other.

Turning off the car, Becca hurriedly scrolled through her contact list. A moment later, Lyndsay Whittmeyer answered with a chirpy hello.

"Hi, Lyndsay. It's Becca. I hate to ask this on such short notice, especially on a school night, but is there any way Marc could sleep over? I'm having a bit of a... situation." This was Cupid's Bow. Lyndsay would hear all about Molly's public intoxication by tomorrow, but Becca didn't have time to get into it now.

"Of course. Coop's baseball game went into extra innings, and we're on our way back from Turtle, but we'll swing by and get Marc just as soon as we can."

"Thanks! You're a lifesaver." Becca disconnected with a mental promise to make a batch of her friend's favorite pecan bars in the very near future. She opened her door. *Time to get this over with.*

She briskly crossed the lot. "Deputy Thomas—"

"Great." Molly stumbled, propping herself up on

the hood of the deputy's car. "My big shister comes bargin' in."

"I'm not 'barging' anywhere. I'm your ride."

The deputy stepped between them, his expression sympathetic and his voice soft. "I got a cup of coffee in her, ma'am. Not sure it's done much good yet. She's…in a state."

"I'll make sure she doesn't end up in this state again," Becca vowed. "Come on, Molly. We're going home."

"Your home," the girl slurred. "Your rules. It's ridicu…it's rid…it's *stupid*!"

Becca took her by the arm, trying to keep her steady. Molly pitched to the left, and they almost went over.

Gritting her teeth, Becca recovered her balance. "How did you even buy drinks? Fake ID?" Most of the bartenders could spot them, especially Jace Trent, who'd been coached by his brother, the sheriff. Plus Molly was supposed to have been with Vicki. Everyone around here knew Vicki Ross wasn't yet legal drinking age.

"Didn't buy 'em. My friend did."

"Let me guess—a male friend. One older than you."

"*Larry* likes me." She managed to make it an accusation.

I like you. Not so much right at the moment, but there was potential for the two of them to be friends. Or was there? Maybe Becca had been fooling herself about her ability to be a good influence, about their being able to find common ground. She leaned over to make sure Molly's seat belt was buckled properly.

"You don't have it in the slot," she said.

"Can't do anything right for you!" Molly cried, swatting away Becca's attempts to help. "Mama never cared if I finished the last of the cereal! Or smiled at a guy."

Odette didn't care—there was breaking news. And Larry Breelan hadn't been feeding an eighteen-year-old drinks because he'd been hoping for a smile. First thing tomorrow, Becca was calling the sheriff and asking him to kindly go tase the offending Breelan.

"Well, I do care," Becca said. "I care about you not making self-destructive choices. And I care about your future. And I care about how this is going to look to the people in my community." She'd been trying so hard to help Molly make friends, wanting her to know that same sense of belonging Becca felt here in Cupid's Bow.

"You care about the *election*!" Molly smacked her hand on the dashboard. "You're afraid someone might not vote for you because your sister got a little tipsy!"

"You passed *tipsy* four or five exits ago. What happened to Vicki? Did she see you get thrown out? I don't want her worried."

"She went home—said her legs were starting to bother her. I told her I had another ride."

"Larry Breelan?" Forget going through the sheriff; Becca would tase the opportunistic lech herself. "Do you have any idea how—"

"Vicki talked about you all night. How you were there for her when she was in a wheelchair last summer, how you're always there for this town. When the hell are you there for me?"

Since the minute you showed up at my door needing a place to live, you ingrate. Becca had been introducing her to people, giving her rides to and from work, encouraging her to want more for herself. But making those points now would be wasted breath. Her sister was too irrational.

Within seconds, Molly went into a full-on rant about the injustice of life, including how her ex had taken her for granted and how it wasn't fair both of her sisters had met their perfect men. She must be using an alternate definition of perfection, one that included shady real estate deals and divorce.

Needing to be free of the escalating verbal abuse, Becca pulled into the driveway at a crooked angle. Then she dutifully came around the side of the car to help, but Molly shoved at her arm.

Becca took a deep breath, fighting the urge to say something she couldn't take back. *Oh, go ahead. She probably won't remember it in the morning, anyway.*

Molly spilled from the car, unsteady but managing not to face-plant on the driveway.

"Need a hand?" Sawyer's voice came from the porch, and Becca glanced his way, torn between gratitude that he was there and humiliation that he was witnessing this.

"Not you, too!" Molly wailed. "Bad enough I'm *her* pity project." She stomped up to the front porch, removing her shoes as she went. One landed sideways on a step. *Cinderella goes on a bender.*

Becca hurried after her, pausing to ask Sawyer, "Where's Marc? Did he—"

"I got him out of the tub and suggested he read in bed, told you were giving Aunt Molly a ride."

"Could you help him pack a bag with his toothbrush and clothes for tomorrow? He gets to have a rare school-night sleepover. The Whittmeyers are on their way." Recalling how she'd joked about Marc spending too much time at their house made her feel guilty; she was damn lucky to be friends with a family who always had her back.

"On it." Sawyer held the door open for her, then headed up the stairs.

Becca found her sister in the kitchen, trying to pour orange juice and spilling it all over the counter. Molly gave her a look of pure malevolence. "You're outta OJ. Better write it on the damn list."

Retaliation burned on the tip of Becca's tongue, the urge to snap. *And you wonder why Odette didn't want you under her roof and your boyfriend didn't love you? Because you're awful.* "We'll discuss this tomorrow. When you're sober. For now, you need to go sleep this off." *Before I stick your ass on a bus to Oklahoma.*

No. She would not dump this on Courtney the way Odette had always dumped her parenting responsibilities on Becca.

She was a little surprised when Molly actually headed toward the stairs instead of doing something to spite her. Still, she didn't fully trust her sister to get into bed without causing further destruction, so she followed along.

Her presence seemed to enrage Molly. "Go away!"

"It's *my* house."

"Mama?" Marc appeared at the top the staircase, freshly bathed and wearing monster truck pj's. His voice was tremulous, the note in it one she normally heard only after a nightmare or during tornado watches.

Her maternal instincts superseded the rage she was feeling, and she softened her tone. "It's okay, baby. Just go wait with Mr. Sawyer." But this *wasn't* okay, and the fact that her little boy was witnessing any of it made the rage bubble hotter.

"Yeah, be a good little boy, Marc, and do what Mommy says," Molly sneered. She grabbed the newel post at the bottom of the steps, pivoting back toward Becca. "You. You think *I'm* seven, too, but I'm not. And you aren't my mommy. You barely want to be my sister!" She wobbled on the second step.

Becca jerked forward to help. "Be careful."

"*Stop telling me what to do!* I'm. Not. A. Kid."

"Then grow the hell up!" Becca realized she was shaking. She couldn't remember the last time she'd lost her temper.

Molly glared at her, angry tears shimmering in her eyes, and whirled around to resume her climb. She made it three more steps before misjudging one, losing her balance and grappling unsuccessfully for the banister.

Marc gasped as his aunt tumbled to the hardwood floor below, narrowly missing Becca, who'd flattened herself against the wall. Molly shrieked, either in fear or pain, but the scream quickly gave way to sobbing. Becca realized her own cheeks were wet.

Kneeling beside her sister, she gingerly poked and prodded to make sure nothing was broken. "Can you wiggle your fingers? Do you think you can stand?"

Suddenly Sawyer was there, strong and steady, first helping Molly to her feet, then picking her up and carrying her upstairs.

As Becca watched the cowboy she was crazy about disappear into her sister's bedroom, she had to bite back hysterical laughter over how wrong the night had gone.

THE NIGHT AIR was cool, and the relative peace of the neighborhood was a relief after the yelling and tears inside. Sawyer darted a sideways glance at Marc, who wasn't saying much as they waiting on the porch for his friend's family.

"You okay, buddy?"

Marc seemed startled by the question. "I'm not the one who fell."

"Your aunt will be okay. Your mom's taking care of her now." From the noises Molly had started making before he'd backed out of the room, Becca was probably holding Molly's hair back while the girl heaved. Having been in Molly's position himself a time or two, he wasn't without sympathy. Still, he figured a hellacious hangover might make the teenager think twice before reaching for a drink again.

"They're both really mad," Marc said.

"Yeah, but not at you. Brothers and sisters fight sometimes."

"Kenny and Coop call each other names. But Coop is nice. He helps us with math sometimes and got us to the next level of Ultimate Fortress Strike." The little boy stared into the distance. "I don't have a brother. I don't even have a daddy. He went away."

"I'm sorry, kid." *Your dad sounds like a jackass.* "But you've got your mom. And she's special. Having her in your corner is like having three or four parents."

"I only need two." Marc sighed. "Mr. Sawyer?"

"Yeah, buddy?"

"Are you gonna leave, too?"

The lump in Sawyer's throat made it difficult to answer. He hadn't expected so much sadness in Marc's eyes, eyes that were a lot like his mom's. Sawyer hated to let the kid down, but he cared about him far too much to lie. "Yes. You and your mom have been great—everyone in Cupid's Bow has been—but this is your home, not mine."

The boy's lower lip trembled, but he nodded. "Where's your home?"

I don't know. Luckily, the Whittmeyers pulled into the driveway before Sawyer was forced to explain that.

How could he summarize his life in a way that made sense to a seven-year-old when Sawyer himself was starting to have questions he couldn't answer?

MRS. WHITTMEYER KEPT knocking on the door to Kenny and Coop's room to check on the boys. That's what she claimed, anyway. "You boys okay? You boys need anything?" But they all knew she was really checking on Marc, peering down at him in a way that made him wish he could shrink into the beanbag chair the same way turtles hid in their shells.

He started to tell her he was fine, just so she'd stop looking at him like that, but Kenny interrupted. "Marc's sad. Brownies would cheer him up."

She was quiet for a moment. "All right—I'll whip up a batch, but after that, you guys have to go to bed. School tomorrow."

Once she was gone, Kenny grinned from the other beanbag. "Video games and brownies on a school night! This is the best."

"Uh-huh." Marc tried to smile.

Coop glanced over from the homework he was doing at his desk. "Wait. Are you *actually* sad?"

Marc shrugged. Tonight had been a little scary. He didn't like seeing Mama mad or seeing Aunt Molly fall, but Sawyer promised his aunt would be okay. What made Marc's tummy hurt was the rest of the conversation he'd had with Sawyer. *I don't want brownies*. He just wanted the cowboy to stay.

"I think Mama likes Mr. Sawyer." She was different with him here. Still Mama, with her rules and her election stress, but Sawyer made her laugh. She said yes to more stuff, like milk shakes and bath crayons. And Trouble! *I have a dog.* Before Sawyer came, Marc had asked if he could have a pet about a million times. She always said no.

"Does the idea of her dating bother you?" Coop asked. "Some of the kids at my middle school have divorced parents, and it can be a difficult transition—"

"Shut up!" Kenny tossed a pillow at his brother. "I hate when you try to talk like a grown-up."

"It's called *maturity*, butt face."

"I wouldn't mind if she dates Mr. Sawyer," Marc said. "But how can she if he's leaving town? He doesn't want to stay in Cupid's Bow."

"That's dumb," Kenny said. "Cupid's Bow is great."

Coop put his chin on his hand. "He just needs a reason to stay."

Marc had learned in social studies that there was a president and a vice president; even the school had a principal and a vice principal. Was there such a thing as a vice mayor? Maybe Sawyer could work for Mama after she won.

Coop rolled back his chair—it was the cool kind with wheels on it, the same as the one Marc sat in when he was at his mom's office. "You said she likes Sawyer. Does *he* like *her*?"

Marc shrugged. "How do you tell? He doesn't take her flowers or kiss her or anything."

Kenny always made throw-up sounds when his parents kissed, but Marc didn't mind if his mama wanted to kiss Mr. Sawyer. Daddy was never coming back, but sometimes Marc still wanted a family. A family like Kenny and Coop had, with two parents who fought sometimes but who also made each other laugh and snuggled together.

"Does he wear a lot of stinky body spray?" Kenny pinched his nose. "That's what Coop does when he likes a girl."

"Hey, Angie Heller said I smelled great when I took her to the Spring Fling dance. That gives me an idea," Coop said excitedly. "Last Halloween, a bunch of us watched a slasher movie. Angie got so scared she buried her face in my shoulder. I think that's when she started liking me. Does your mom ever watch horror movies?"

"Never."

"I got it!" Kenny snapped his fingers, which used to make Marc jealous, because he couldn't do it right. But Kenny couldn't whistle, so they were even. "You can borrow Slither. Your mom's afraid of snakes. If we let Slither loose in your house, Sawyer can capture him and your mom will be so happy she might kiss him or something."

Maybe—but Marc would be grounded for a *long* time. Like, until he was older than Coop. Or even Aunt Molly. "I don't think that will work. Besides, I have a dog now." He sat a little taller in his beanbag. "A real good dog. If Trouble saw a snake in the house, she'd probably kill it to protect us." Dogs could do a lot more than snakes could.

"I think grown-ups have to go on dates to see if they like each other," Coop said.

"That's dumb." Kenny had a long list of things that were dumb. "Why would you even go if you didn't like a person? Hi, I hate you, wanna have a date?"

Coop ignored his brother. "If Sawyer takes her to dinner or asks her to dance, you'll know he likes her."

And then he might stay. Marc grinned for the first time since Mrs. Whittmeyer had picked him up.

Life had been interesting lately, which was nice, but if Sawyer stayed with Mama, life just might be perfect.

BECCA STOOD AT the bottom of the spiral staircase. She and Sawyer still had an important conversation to finish. Besides, she wanted to thank him again for his help. Only lingering embarrassment stalled her. The Baker girls had not been at their best tonight.

You're not a Baker anymore.

Oh, but she was. She was beginning to realize she always would be. That her recent quest to have voters see her in a positive light had actually begun years ago, when an awkwardly tall, poor girl had yearned for the respect of her classmates and teachers. Was her need to distance herself from that past why she'd kept her married name after Colin had bailed on their marriage? Even as a jilted wife who'd been publicly humiliated, Becca Johnston had been a step up from Rebecca Baker. "Mayor Johnston" would be still further from those humble beginnings, but winning the election wouldn't change who her family was.

And fidgeting pointlessly at the bottom of the steps wouldn't change what Sawyer had witnessed tonight. Lifting her chin, she started climbing the stairs.

The soft, bluesy strains of a guitar drifted from his room; she assumed he was listening to the radio or an iPod. It wasn't until she stood outside his door, which was cracked open a few inches, that she realized *he* was playing. He sat on the bed in a white undershirt and jeans, an acoustic guitar across his lap. Apparently the calluses on his long, capable fingers weren't just from ranch work.

The notes trailed off as he glanced up, meeting her gaze.

"Sorry to interrupt," she said, wishing he hadn't stopped. Watching him had been mesmerizing, especially the expression on his face, somewhere between bliss and concentration. It was easy to imagine him with the same rapt focus when he was touching a woman, bringing her pleasure as unerringly as he'd brought those soulful chords to life.

"No apology necessary," he said. "I left the door open so I could hear you if you needed me. Is she doing better?"

"She's passed out cold." Arguably an improvement over vomit-rama, which had been so gross Becca had gone for a hot shower after she had her sister changed into clean clothes. Now she stood in Sawyer's room in a silky pajama set, her damp hair drying in ringlets over her shoulder. Given their early morning kitchen encounters, this was far from the first time he'd seen her in pj's. But being alone in his bedroom with him felt a lot different than leaning against the counter as they both waited for the coffeemaker to finish.

The attic itself seemed cozier than usual in the muted light of matched lamps, with the house quiet below. It was at once peaceful and charged with an electric tension that built with each step she took toward him. Ignoring the two chairs she passed, she sat next to him on the bed. The mattress creaked a soft whisper of greeting and Sawyer welcomed her with that too-appealing tilted smile. She had the impulse to trace her thumb over his lips.

Instead, she nodded toward the guitar. "I didn't know you played." There was a lot she didn't know about him. And yet she felt so close to him, able to confide in him as if he were a friend, repeatedly trusting him with her son.

He regarded the pale wooden guitar as if seeing it for the first time. "This was my brother Charlie's. He asked for it for Christmas his freshman year of high school, took lessons for a few months. But then he got hyperfocused on school and keeping his GPA scholarship-worthy. The guitar ended up in the hall closet, and I stumbled across it when I was bored one rainy afternoon. Taught myself with the help of the workbook he'd left in the case and some online videos."

"Your parents must have been glad the investment wasn't wasted." She was speaking as someone who was financially responsible for things like piano lessons, but immediately wished she'd said something warmer, like, "your parents must be proud of your talent."

He made a noncommittal noise, dropping his gaze as he strummed the strings. "Got any requests?"

"Not really. Just no songs about booze tonight." Dread slithered through her as she thought about how many people had been at the dance hall and how many more would hear about it tomorrow. "I know it's self-centered to take this personally, to worry about how Molly might make *me* look, but with Truitt scrambling for reasons to skewer me..." She forced a tight smile, trying not to borrow trouble. "But every family has its troublemakers, right?"

"My family sure did. You're looking at him."

"Were you really that bad?" She tried to imagine him as a hell-raising young man. There was always a hint of wickedness in Sawyer's smile, but he was also someone who helped with second-grade homework and assisted little old ladies with car trouble.

"I guess 'bad' depends on your perspective. As a kid, I was a prankster. It probably started because I wanted to be just like Charlie. We had practical joke battles right up until April Fool's Day of his sophomore year in college. Harder to organize pranks long-distance, but we were creative."

The affection in his tone made her feel wistful. She and her own siblings hadn't shared that kind of bond— which shouldn't depress her, because she didn't even like pranks. People could get hurt. Yet it was obvious he and his brother had been close.

"Then Charlie buckled down, got serious and made the dean's list. I was proud of him—we all were. Until he graduated with a bachelor's degree in pompous arrogance. With honors. I'd always thought, as my dad got older, that Charlie and I would run the ranch together. But it was…challenging after he came home. I decided to strike out on my own. I worked ranches, accumulated rodeo wins. There were wild nights that I cannot, as a gentleman, discuss."

Becca didn't want a gentleman tonight. She wanted to relive the gripping passion she'd felt this morning when she'd thought he might kiss her; she wanted to blot out the last few hours, put aside her tangled relationship with her family and explore how good she and Sawyer could be together.

"I never had the chance to be a troublemaker," she said. "I was busy taking care of my younger brothers and sisters, my son, this town. Don't get me wrong, I'm no martyr—I love Marc and I love Cupid's Bow. But trying to be good for everyone gets exhausting." She trailed her fingers over his collarbone.

He inhaled sharply, but otherwise didn't react.

She closed the distance between them, her pulse erratic and her voice low. "Don't I deserve the chance to be bad?"

Chapter Eleven

Knowing how direct Becca was, Sawyer shouldn't have been so surprised when she pressed her lips to his. Yet for just a moment, he couldn't believe this was happening.

Need sparked through him as he breathed in the scent of her skin, registered the warmth of her soft curves through his clothes. *Yes.* Yes, this was really happening. He cupped the nape of her neck, angling her head to deepen the kiss. Gently at first, so he didn't rush her.

But then she threaded her fingers through his hair, tugged him closer and knocked his world sideways.

Damn, the woman could kiss. His heart pounded faster with each beat, and desire pounded through him even harder. She sucked at his lower lip, and he went almost light-headed with desire. Had he pushed her down on the mattress or had she pulled him across her? When had they gone horizontal?

He groaned, trying to pull back from her addictive mouth long enough to assess the situation. "This is moving fast."

"And fast is bad?" she asked coyly.

I don't know. Selfish desire warred with concern for her.

Her smile faltered, and she propped herself up on her elbows. "Do you not want…"

"Are you kidding me, woman? I'm hard-pressed to think of anything I've ever wanted more." He glanced pointedly at his lap. "*Very* hard-pressed. But you've had an emotional night. I don't want to take advantage."

She sat up, her fingers skimming beneath the hem of his thin shirt. "Okay, now I want you even more. I appreciate the concern—and it has been an emotional night—but I wasn't upset when I wanted you to kiss me this morning. Or when I wanted to touch you in the kitchen, before we were interrupted. You've thought about it, too, right?"

He leaned forward to kiss a path from the curve of her neck to her cleavage. "Sweetheart, I've barely been able to think of anything else since the first time I saw you."

She gave a murmur of approval at his words, arching her back when he palmed one breast through her top. "I want this," she said breathlessly. Her body gave him the same message, her nipples hard against the satiny material of her pajamas, her hips subtly rocking against his, beckoning him closer.

Eager to accommodate, he unbuttoned the sleep shirt, baring her generous breasts. He rubbed his thumb across one peak, feeling both reverent and possessive. When he bent down to replace his thumb with his tongue, she made a sharp, sexy sound, so he did it again.

He wanted to give her everything, wanted to make her shake with desire. "Tell me what you want."

"You." She shuddered as he licked and suckled her. "Wait, there is one other thing…"

"Name it."

Her voice was pure seduction. "Can I be on top?"

With a grin, he rolled over. "You do like to be in charge, don't you?"

She straddled him. "Don't worry, cowboy. I'll make sure you like it, too."

Becca woke disoriented to predawn birdsong outside the window, stiffening when realization hit her. *I'm naked! I'm naked in Sawyer's bed!*

Well, technically, she owned the bed. And the house. Which would make leaving easy—she only had to go down one flight of stairs—but could make everything else awkward. There would definitely be no avoiding each other. Not that she *wanted* to avoid him, necessarily. She didn't regret any of the three times they'd had sex throughout the night, each one better than the last. But being in the same house didn't give her time or space to process what had happened.

"I know you aren't a morning person," Sawyer murmured, without raising his face from the pillow next to her, "So I'm trying not to take your panic as an insult."

"Panic? Who's panicking?"

"I've been to petrified forests where the wood isn't as rigid as you are right now. Do you want to talk about it?"

She expelled a breath, vastly reassured. He was just as wonderful now as he had been last night. "Not really. But it means a lot that you offered. I don't want you to think I have regrets. It's just been a long time since I woke up next to a man. And I've never woken up next to any man except for Marc's father."

Sawyer sat up, his expression perplexed. "You mean since the divorce."

"I mean since ever." She'd slept only with her ex-husband. In high school, she'd never even been tempted. Growing up with a mother who was habitually pregnant had left Becca convinced that the reward wouldn't be worth the risk. "Colin and I married young. And before that, I was too worried about the possibility of accidental pregnancy. You may have noticed I was very adamant about the condoms."

He chuckled. "That's not the part of last night that stands out in my memory."

"It was all pretty memorable." She sighed. "In a perfect world, I could stay and we could do it again, but I have work. Plus, I should check on Molly. And call the Whittmeyers to make sure Marc is all right."

"I'll bet he's hanging in there—you're raising a great kid. Will I see you tonight?"

"Unless I miraculously turn invisible. I live here, remember?"

He smirked. "Ha-ha. I meant—"

"I knew what you meant," she said softly. Would there be any repeat of this, of them together? "Marc will be back home tonight, and my current relationship with my sister is…volatile, to say the least. I'd like to set good examples for both of them."

"So no cuddling on the couch, making out in the stairwell or throwing you down on the kitchen table?"

Her face heated. "That was a joke, right? I mean, it's not something you've actually thought about while we're sitting there having coffee?"

"No comment."

Damn. Now *she* would be thinking about that the next time they were in the kitchen together. "I have to be discreet. As for when I might find myself up here again… Can we play it by ear?"

"Of course." He pulled her close, kissing her shoulder. "You know where to find me."

Before Becca left for work, she hadn't been able to get any response from the motionless lump that was her sister. So she'd left water, aspirin and a note saying she'd check back later on the nightstand. She returned on her lunch break, after the most productive morning she'd had in months; either sex left her energized or she was working *really* hard in order to avoid thinking about last night. She wasn't ashamed of anything they'd done, but she was in the habit of thinking long-term. With Sawyer, that thought process was null.

Luckily, she had plenty of other things to concentrate on—like a full-time job, a town-wide celebration, a debate in three days and a pain-in-the-ass sister.

When she pulled up in front of the house, Sawyer's truck was gone. He'd mentioned exploring a fort today for a piece he was writing that included a lot of the area's history. She was both relieved she and her sister wouldn't have an audience within earshot of their conversation, and paradoxically disappointed not to see him.

After letting Trouble out, she went to Molly's room with a bowl of soup; she'd stopped to buy a couple cans on the way home.

"Knock, knock," she said, not shouting, but making

no effort to keep her voice down, either. If Molly had a killer headache, that was her own fault.

Molly mumbled something unintelligible.

Becca put the soup on the nightstand. "I don't mean to be a hard-ass about this, but I need you to wake up. There are some things we have to discuss before Marc comes home this afternoon."

"Oh, God." Molly shoved a tangle of hair out her face. "Marc. I was awful to him."

"You were awful to everyone," Becca said matter-of-factly. "But you can't ever do that again in front of my son. If you do, you're out."

Molly nodded silently, her eyes glittering with tears. After a moment, she reached for the tissues on the nightstand, sniffling. "You love him so much. Do you think…do you think our mother ever loved us?"

The question caught Becca off guard. "Yes." In the beginning, maybe, when they were snuggly babies and not unruly toddlers or kids with increasingly complicated lives. Odette liked cradling newborns, but in the years that followed, she was crap at parenting. When Becca was young, it had never occurred to her to question why her mother kept having babies. They'd lived in a rural town surrounded by family-owned farms, with a predominantly Catholic population. Large families were not uncommon. Looking back, though, Becca wondered if their mother had been trying to recapture that early love she'd felt for her children.

I'll probably never know. While Becca had made her peace with that, it was clear Molly was still tormented by her upbringing, by questions of whether she'd been wanted. There was one certainty Becca could give her sister. "Daddy loved us…so much. He *adored* you. There were complications when the twins were born, and I don't think he ever expected to be a father again after that. Then you came. I remember how excited he was when they brought you home from the hospital. I wish you could've known him longer."

"Me, too. I only have a few memories, but they're all good. I feel like my happiest childhood moments were with him."

"Do you think… Is that maybe why you're drawn to older men?" Becca asked gently. Maybe once Molly identified the underlying cause of her actions, it would be easier to change her behavior.

But Molly recoiled, her face tight with anger. "That is *gross*! And you don't know what you're talking about. Who died and made you a licensed therapist?"

"I'm sorry. I—"

"Out." Molly grabbed the plastic wastebasket Becca had left next to the bed, brandishing it in front of her like a weapon. "I'm gonna be sick again. So unless you want to stay and watch…"

Hell, no. After last night, she never wanted to hear the sound of retching again. Yet it seemed important that Molly know she wasn't alone. "If you need me, I'll stay."

Her sister looked startled by the offer, but then waved her hand in a shooing motion. "No. You should go."

With a nod, Becca turned toward the door, touched when Molly added quietly, "But thank you."

BECAUSE MOLLY CALLED in sick to work Friday, everyone was home that night. The mood was odd—not tense, in Becca's opinion, but unnaturally subdued. Marc was quiet through dinner; Lyndsay had admitted on the phone that she'd probably let the boys stay up too late. Molly had insisted on joining them at the table, as if it was some kind of penance, dining on weak tea and crackers without saying much. Sawyer was...

Actually, Becca had no idea what Sawyer was doing or thinking, because she'd barely allowed herself to look at him all evening. She was paranoid her smiles or glances would reveal too much, that anyone who saw them together would somehow know they'd been intimate. Ridiculous, yet she couldn't quite shake the irrational fear.

It wasn't until after dinner, when Molly retreated to her room and Marc took the puppy out, that Becca felt comfortable enough to address Sawyer directly. Even then, she kept her gaze on the dinner dishes she was scrubbing furiously, rather than make eye contact.

"I'm not trying to ignore you," she apologized.

"I know." His tone was amused, affectionate.

Still, she felt bad for giving him what a less understanding man might deem the cold shoulder. "This is all so new to me and I'm having trouble acting natural, but it doesn't mean you've done anything wrong or—"

"I know, Becca." He gently squeezed the nape of her neck, and she almost jumped.

She glanced back, meaning to smile at him, but frowned instead. "You're taking this awfully well." Because he'd had so many affairs he could be sophisticated and blasé about having seen her naked?

"I'm not taking it nearly as well as you think. I wanted to kiss you all through dinner, wanted to call you a least a dozen times today, and of course, there's that kitchen table right there..."

She followed his gaze, her pulse quickening as she recalled his words this morning. She couldn't remember ever having had fantasies about doing it on the table, but she was pretty sure there were some in her future.

"But," he continued, "you indicated this morning that you needed a little time to adjust. The last time I backed off and let you come to me, it worked out *very* well." He gave her a lazy grin that didn't mask the predatory gleam in his eyes. "Gives a man hope."

She smiled back, but knew that hope of his wouldn't be paid off tonight. She was spending the evening with Marc and planned to stay close by if he needed her—no sneaking up to the attic. "You may have a little bit of a wait."

His gaze darted back and forth, and once he'd ensured there were no witnesses, he ducked in for a lightning-quick kiss, over before it began, but still enough to make her tremble. "You're worth it."

When Marc came back inside, Sawyer made small talk with him for a few minutes and then excused himself, gracefully giving Becca the space she needed. *He's damn near perfect.* Except for the pesky leaving-in-a week part. She decided not to think about it.

"Mama, when are we going to hear the TV lady sing?" Marc asked.

"You mean the concert? Day after tomorrow. Are you looking forward to it?"

Marc nodded, but he seemed more dismissive than excited. "Is Mr. Sawyer coming with us?"

"Yep." She'd given him one of her VIP tickets.

"Maybe since there's music, you should dance with him."

She frowned at the uncharacteristic suggestion, trying to remember if she'd ever heard him mention dancing before. Where was this coming from? "I suppose it's a possibility." Maybe if she danced with a couple different people, so it didn't look as if she was singling him out…

Did Sawyer like to dance? He was a rodeo champion, so he obviously liked physical recreation. And after last night, she could attest that he had a keen sense of rhythm.

"Did you and Daddy ever used to dance?"

This line of questioning was getting weirder; Marc rarely ever mentioned his dad. "We did at our wedding. Would you like to look at the photo album sometime?"

While she personally didn't want to dwell on her romance with Colin, she didn't want to erase Marc's sense of having a father…even if Colin had been more a figurehead than a hands-on parent. He'd showed up to play proud dad at T-ball games and church choir concerts, had always smiled brightly in their family Christmas photo, but when it came to the nitty-gritty of their daily lives? Becca had run everything, from selecting the pediatrician to deciding Marc's bedtime and extracurricular activities. In retrospect, she was ashamed that she had never pushed Colin to take a bigger role. Because she'd liked being in charge, it hadn't bothered her. Colin worked long hours to support their family, and she'd thought the two of them were simply playing to their strengths. If she'd encouraged him to spend more time bonding with his child, would he have stayed for Marc's sake?

Shaking off the past, she smiled brightly at her son. *I'll just have to love him enough for both of us.* "Why the sudden interest in dancing? Want me to teach you how it's done?"

He backed away, looking vaguely horrified. "No, I just thought *you* might like to dance. With Mr. Sawyer."

Wait, was this her seven-year-old trying to play matchmaker? "I'll ask him about it," she said neutrally. If the concert were in a neighboring county where she didn't know anyone, she'd like nothing better than to spend the evening in Sawyer's arms.

But here in Cupid's Bow? She'd been insisting to others that he was a tenant and nothing more; if she snuggled up to him publicly, she'd get some serious side eye. Well, except maybe from Amy Prescott, who'd probably just want to high-five her.

"Honey, you know that Mr. Sawyer isn't my...boyfriend, right?" *No, definitely not a boyfriend, just my secret lover.* Guilt suffused her. Was she a terrible mom for sleeping with a man she'd known only a week?

Marc didn't answer. "I'm going to get the checkerboard. You said you'd play after dinner," he reminded her.

She nodded, glad they weren't playing anything more mentally taxing. Her thoughts had been jumbled all day, and now she had new worries. She was glad her son thought so highly of Sawyer, but she didn't want to give him false hopes. He'd already been abandoned by his father; if Sawyer broke his heart, the kid might end up needing therapy.

Thinking of her conversation earlier with Molly, about their childhood and whether or not their mom had loved them, Becca sighed inwardly. *Frankly, we could all benefit from a little counseling.* Maybe they could get a group discount.

"HATE TO SAY I told you so," Brody said with faux sympathy, "but I don't think your landlady likes you. At all."

"Is that so?" Sawyer tipped back his straw cowboy hat and pulled a handkerchief from his back pocket to wipe the sweat off his face. This morning's sun, though warm, had been bearable; the afternoon temperatures weren't playing so nicely. Oh, this would be nice enough weather for fishing on the shaded bank of a river or napping in a hammock—preferably with Becca cuddled against him—but the last few hours of assembling booths and makeshift stages for the festival had been grueling manual labor.

Brody put down the toolbox he'd carried over from the other side of town square. "Well, she's bossing all of us around—it's Becca way—but she *really* seems to have it in for you."

Sawyer grinned inwardly, thinking of how flustered she'd been that morning when they'd had their customary encounter by the coffeepot. She'd started to admit that she'd had a dream about him last night, but had abruptly cut herself off, cheeks reddening. *She likes me just fine.* In fact, he'd love to tell his friend about what had happened—not because he wanted to brag about going to bed with her, but simply because she hovered in his thoughts constantly. Being unable to share any of those thoughts was stifling.

Before the two of them had left the house that morning, Becca had reiterated that it was important everyone see them as platonic, for Marc's sake. Recalling how vulnerable the kid had seemed when he'd asked if Sawyer was going away, Sawyer had readily agreed to play it cool in public.

Becca, however, was overcompensating. She was an all-or-nothing woman, and acting casual was clearly not in her repertoire. First there'd been her refusal to so much as glance at him at dinner. Now she was going out of her way not to show him any favoritism, even though he was the only nonlocal who'd volunteered to help set up the festival. Last night he'd been amused by her terrible show of feigned indifference. Today, he was...oddly aroused. Turned out there were times he could appreciate a bossy woman, especially when he vividly recalled her climbing atop him two nights ago.

Besides, her determination to keep him busy made him feel like part of the inner circle. The longest break he'd had all day was the last thirty seconds, which was akin to how she ran Molly's and Marc's lives. She meant well, trying to keep Molly out of trouble and wanting Marc to be well-rounded with his music lessons and sports and junior civic duties. It was hard to fault her intentions, even if Sawyer didn't particularly agree with her methods. In her own manic, she-should-probably-cut-back-on-caffeine kind of way, keeping people active was how she showed she cared.

Now, if only the rest of the town realized that.

While Brody's heckling about her was more of a running joke than a real accusation, some of the other volunteers were grumbling about how hard Becca was working them.

An hour later, waiting for his turn to fill a cup of water from the cooler, Sawyer tried to defend her. "She has a fun side," he protested.

A bald, burly man in a Cupid's Bow Fire Department T-shirt raised his eyebrows. "Who are you, again? And how do you know Becca?"

"Sawyer McCall." He shook the man's hand. "I've been renting a room from her for the past week."

"Ah. Maybe she's more relaxed at home," the man said skeptically, "but my cousin worked at the community center last summer, said Becca is a total perfectionist."

"That would be a good quality in a mayor," Sawyer said. "You know she'd never do a half-assed job."

"But a big part of the job is being able to work with others. If she alienates everyone, how will she get anything done? Assuming she can even win the election."

"It'll be close." Manuel Diaz, who'd introduced himself to Sawyer that morning, reached for the paper cups stacked next to the ice water. "But she has my vote. Sierra's been telling all of us at the hospital what a great job Becca will do. It may come down to the small business owners—they're the backbone of the town's economy, and Truitt's been wooing them with grand promises. I hope they keep in mind on voting day how few of those promises he kept this term."

The bald man grinned. "Damn, Manny, didn't realize you were so interested in local politics. Maybe you should be on the town council."

Manuel chuckled. "Sierra and my girlfriend both say that, too."

After that, conversation turned to local gossip and Sawyer walked away with a polite nod, sipping his water and thinking over everything he'd heard. He wouldn't be in Cupid's Bow much longer, but maybe he could do some good while he was here.

SAWYER SAT BEHIND the steering wheel, watching through the windshield as Becca finished talking to an elderly lady in a Houston Astros shirt, and a short bearded man. Even though Sawyer was tired and ready for a shower, he didn't mind the wait—not when he had this view of sunlight shining on Becca's red-gold hair or the sway of her body as she gestured. But then she turned toward the truck, and he dropped his gaze so that he wasn't caught staring.

"Sorry I took so long," she said as she climbed in.

"No worries. You did warn me, after all."

When he'd suggested riding into town together, she'd originally declined, pointing out that, as festival chair, she might have to stay longer. Wanting time alone with her—even if it was just the fifteen-minute ride back to the house—he'd told her he'd wait if necessary. He'd eventually cajoled her into agreeing, teasingly reminding her that one vehicle was better for the environment than two, and she had voters to impress.

Speaking of which... What was the best way to tell her about the brainstorm he'd had earlier?

Her head fell back against the seat. All day, she'd projected an image of being in charge, reassuring people who came to her with problems, and "motivating" would-be slackers to get the job done right. Now she sighed, her expression showing hints of vulnerability. "I'm exhausted."

Oh, boy. That might make tonight a less-than-ideal time for the houseguests he was about to spring on her. But it was still early evening. "Think you have time for a nap before dinner?"

She stifled a yawn. "If I lay down now, it would be too hard to get back up."

"I worry about you running yourself ragged." It was almost enough to make him feel guilty about that third time they'd had sex Thursday night, and how little sleep she'd gotten. *Almost.*

"Things are just crazy right now, with the centennial and the mayoral campaign," she said. "I'll catch up on my rest after the election."

He snorted. "After the election, you'll be too busy running the town."

"Then I'll delegate someone on my staff to take naps for me." She reached over to squeeze his hand, and he wanted to stop the truck and kiss her. "You really think I'm going to win?"

She would if he had anything to say about it. "You know how you've said I should feel free to use the common areas?" She'd told him to make himself at home in the living room and kitchen, so long as he cleaned up after himself and respected her policy about grocery inventory.

She frowned at the non sequitur. "Sure."

"And you meant it, right?"

"Yes." But she said it warily.

"Great—because I invited a few people over tonight."

"Tonight?" Her voice was shrill, one might even say edged with panic. She took a deep breath. "How many is 'a few'?"

"Four or five. Enough for a rousing game of poker at the kitchen table."

She pinched the bridge of her nose. "And it had to be tonight? The festival kicks off tomorrow, and I'm trying to prepare for the debate on Monday."

And he wanted to help. If tonight went well, maybe

there'd be a few more friendly faces in the audience at that debate. "I promise my motives aren't selfish—they're political."

She laughed. "Cynics would say those usually go hand in hand."

"You know Manuel Diaz, right?" At her nod, he added, "He thinks some of the local business owners could be very important in this election. But you have a certain...reputation in town. For being..."

"Controlling? Bossy? This is Sierra's posters all over again," she muttered.

"Whose what?"

"My friend Sierra. She works with Manny in physical therapy at the hospital. You wouldn't believe what she wanted to put on the campaign posters."

"Becca Johnston for Global Domination?"

She rolled her eyes. "Vote for Our Favorite Control Freak. As I told her, there's nothing freakish about being organized."

"You are not a freak of any kind. You're smart. And determined. And funny. And bighearted." He could name a dozen more things he loved about her—but it wasn't his good opinion she needed. "But it's possible some people in town haven't had a glimpse behind the public image yet, at the real you. So I invited Manny, who's already on your side, and a few men in town he thinks are influential."

"Just men, huh? I'll have you know, women can be excellent poker players. In college, I won enough one semester to pay for all my textbooks."

"For the record, I also asked two women, but neither of them could make it on such short notice. Thank

God you play, because this will work a lot better if you join us."

"Why would anyone decide to vote for me just because I play a couple hands of poker with him?" She clenched her jaw. "If you think for a second I'm going to let someone win—"

"Nah, I would never ask that of you." And he wouldn't respect her half as much if she stooped to that kind of manipulation. "Be yourself. Just don't gloat too much if you kick our asses."

"I make no promises."

Chapter Twelve

Manny rose from his chair, looking toward the dealer. "Count me out this round—I have an early morning." He flashed a teasing smile. "Plus, I've lost all the money I can afford to for one night."

Becca checked her watch. "I actually have to leave to pick up Molly in about fifteen minutes, anyway."

As people stood around the table, Sawyer allowed himself a self-congratulatory smile. Tonight had turned out even better than he'd expected. Not financially—he was down nineteen bucks—but for Becca. He watched her now, as she joked with the editor of the local newspaper, the *Cupid's Bow Clarion*. She looked relaxed and happy...and thirty dollars richer. Conversation had centered around the festival and some good-natured trash talking.

As a scowling Roger Sands approached Becca, however, Sawyer realized that the town councilman was getting less good-natured by the moment. "A Johnston taking my money," the balding man growled. "Just like old times."

Becca stiffened. So did everyone else, eyes on her as the men in the room waited to see how she responded.

Manny took a step closer to Becca, as if preparing to intervene on her behalf.

But she wasn't one to shrink from confrontation. "I'm sorry you lost some money in Colin's last property investment deal," she told Sands, her voice so quiet Sawyer could barely make out the words. "But Marc and I lost more than anyone. Our family—my marriage—fell apart."

Sands lowered his gaze, shamefaced, barely mumbling a goodbye before hustling toward the front door. It banged shut behind him. Once they heard his car start, it was as if everyone else exhaled in relief.

Manny squeezed her shoulder, and Sawyer was surprised by the irrational flash of jealousy that went through him. "This has been fun," the physical therapist said. "It'd be *more* fun if we don't invite Sands next time."

Everyone trickled out with polite farewells, thanking Becca for her hospitality. None of them knew it had been involuntary. Then the house was quiet, with Marc already in bed and Molly still at work.

Becca sighed. "We've never really talked about my ex."

"Do you want to?" Sawyer could be a good listener, if that was what she needed, but she didn't owe him any explanations about her past.

"No. Maybe." She reached for the now-empty bowl of queso on the table and carried it to the sink. "Colin was always ambitious—it was one of the reasons I was attracted to him. But I think that ambition got corrupted somewhere along the line. He convinced people in our community to invest in a resort on the coast, and the whole deal fell apart. When he left, I thought he was embarrassed, that he'd been duped. Took me a while to realize it had been a scam and that he was probably fleeing criminal charges. No one ever found enough evidence to convict him, but thank God I kept my own financial accounts, separate from him and his company. Even now, when I think about it, I feel so stu—"

"Hey." Sawyer pulled her into a hug. "*You* didn't do anything wrong."

"Except fall in love with a fraud."

If Sawyer had felt a prick of jealousy over Manny's casual contact, it was nothing compared to the wave that swamped him hearing her say she loved another man. *Of course she loved him—he was her damn husband.* Maybe what bothered him wasn't the statement of the obvious so much as the realization that he would never hear her say she loved *him*.

His stomach clenched, knotted in a riot of conflicting emotions. He'd barely even considered the prospect of a steady girlfriend before; he had little experience with commitment. He couldn't really want a single mom—and prospective mayor—to fall in love with him. That was commitment squared.

Becca pulled away, her voice soft. "Do you think I'm running for mayor because deep down I want to prove I still have the town's respect? I tell myself I have noble goals, but what if this is just a way to distance myself from what Colin did?"

"You love Cupid's Bow. No one who's talked to you for more than five minutes could ever doubt that. And, okay, maybe you also have some personal motivation, but so what? As long as you do the best job you can for the community, does it really matter what prompted you to run?" Her ex had ruined enough for her and Marc without also making her second-guess her campaign. *Bastard.* "Too bad you don't know where he is—I'd be willing to rearrange his face."

Becca gave him a sunny smile. "You'd have to get in line behind me."

"LITTLE KNOWN FACT—concerts are actually supposed to be fun."

The rollicking chorus of Kylie Jo's latest hit made it practically impossible to hear conversation. But Sawyer had murmured his teasing reprimand right at Becca's ear, close enough for his breath to feather over her skin, and she shivered at the sensation. It was so tempting to lean back and let her body melt into his.

Instead, she stood straight, hoping their nearness only made them look like two people crowded together in front of the stage, not like two people who'd seen each other naked.

"I am having fun," she said. More or less. The songs were upbeat and she did her best to clap along with everyone else, while also mentally reviewing for tomorrow night's debate, keeping an eye on Marc, who was a few yards away with Kenny Whittmeyer, and trying to find Molly in the surrounding crowd. She'd said she was going to get a soda; Becca wanted to make damn sure her sister didn't get distracted by a beer vendor or a Breelan.

Sawyer placed his hand on the nape of her neck, pressing with his thumb and rotating it in a slow circle that made her moan.

"That feels incredible," she said, her body sagging against his despite her resolve.

"You're tense. What are you doing later tonight?"

he whispered, his voice coaxing. "I could give you an excellent full body massage. You need to relax."

Reluctantly, she took a step away from him. "What I need is to work on my to-do list. Tomorrow is—"

"Delegate," he suggested. "Make sure you leave a little time for you. By which I mean *us*."

Her breath caught. It was such a seductive idea— that she and Sawyer were a united "them." But there were only a few days until the trail ride, where they would be surrounded by others. Becca would never risk sneaking into his tent, and after the trail ride, he was leaving. *I can count on one hand the number of nights we have left together.* The realization ached in her chest.

She swallowed hard, changing the subject. "Do you see Molly anywhere?"

His sigh sounded exasperated.

"What?" Craning her head, she turned to look at him. "What's wrong?"

"Nothing." A moment later, he gave her a half-hearted smile. "But it's a slap to the ego that I'm trying to put the moves on you and you're more interested in what your sister is doing. She's eighteen. She can find her own way to the concession stand and back."

"You think I'm overprotective."

"I... It's really none of my business." He glanced toward the stage, where the band was finishing up the song Kylie Jo had won the TV competition with. "And this probably isn't the place to discuss it, anyway."

Though Becca nodded, she continued to think about what he'd said. Yes, technically Molly was an adult. But hadn't he seen how much trouble she'd gotten herself into less than a week ago? Becca had cause to worry.

"Hey, Mrs. Johnston!"

As the opening guitar notes of a ballad played, she glanced down to find Kenny and Marc. "Hey, guys— having a good time?"

Her son nodded. "But we're hungry. Can I have a waffle cone?"

"Is Mrs. W. going to stand in line with you? I don't want you wandering in this crowd without an adult."

"Coop said he'd take us," Kenny chimed in.

"Then I guess—"

"Mama!" Marc tugged on the lace-edged sleeve of her peasant blouse. "This song is so slow even *you* could dance to it."

Ouch. If Sawyer wanted to experience a real slap to the ego, he should try parenting. Kids were hell on the old self-esteem.

Marc had redirected his focus to the cowboy. "Do you like dancing, Mr. Sawyer?"

He smiled. "I guess there's only one way to find out. Becca?"

"Oh, but I don't..." She couldn't bring herself to say no—not when she so badly wanted to be in his arms. So she gave her son a ten-dollar bill for ice cream and, as the boys scampered away, laced her fingers with Sawyer's.

He pulled her close, and need sizzled through her. Aside from a few stolen kisses at the house, he hadn't really touched her in days. She missed him. How much worse was it going to be after he was gone? They swayed to the music. She should be enjoying herself, loving the way his body brushed hers, but she couldn't relax into the moment. Her mind was racing.

"I know the city is paying you to help with the trail

ride," she said, "and that you win money from the rodeos, but have you ever thought about...something else?" Would he be bored, planting roots in a small town like this one?

"Like what?"

"I don't know." She thought about how moved she'd been reading one of his articles. "Maybe writing a book someday?"

He laughed. "There are days when I curse my way through trying to finish a two-page piece. Not sure a whole manuscript would be for me. That's a hell of a commitment."

Right. "Stupid idea," she muttered. "Forget I said anything."

He tipped her chin up with his finger, studying her face. "What's troubling you, sweetheart?"

Lots of things. But at least she knew how to fix one of them. "Sexual frustration." She went up on her toes so that she could whisper in his ear, "I will definitely be coming upstairs to visit you tonight."

His grip on her tightened, making her smile despite her brief moment of melancholy. "Hot damn. How soon can we get out of here?"

BECCA COULDN'T REMEMBER ever sleeping through her alarm before, but that's exactly what she did on Monday morning. After several wonderful hours spent in Sawyer's room the night before, she'd staggered drowsily to her own bed and crashed into blissful sleep. But when she woke up forty minutes late and caught a glimpse of the time, any remaining bliss wore off in a hurry.

She was frantic as she scurried around the kitchen

while Marc got dressed, shoving coffee filters into his lunch box instead of back into the cabinet where they belonged.

Sawyer shot her a guilty glance from the end of the counter, where he was waiting for caffeine and trying to stifle his yawns. He'd also slept later than usual today, but he wasn't the one who had to get a kid to school, a dog to the vet and a newspaper reporter to the senior center. As part of the centennial week, the paper was interviewing the oldest living citizen in Cupid's Bow, but on her bad days, Miss June confused easily, and Becca wanted to be there to help make sure the interview went smoothly. She wished she could assign that chore to Sawyer—maybe he might be interested in working for a paper someday. It could be a nice steady job that allowed him to settle in one place. But Miss June got flustered around strangers.

Maybe he'd be willing to help with something else; delegating had been his idea, after all. "I hate to ask this of you, but—"

"Sweetheart, after last night, you could ask for one of my kidneys. Or my truck." He cocked his head to the side, considering. "Okay, maybe not the truck. Seriously, just tell me what you need."

"Can you take Trouble to the vet for me this morning?" she asked, as Marc's footsteps thumped down the staircase. He was moving fast, well aware from her half-dozen reminders that they were running late. She bit her lip. "And maybe take Marc to his piano lesson this afternoon? I've got the debate tonight and—"

"Done."

"Thank you." If Marc hadn't been barreling into

the room, she would have kissed Sawyer to show her gratitude. "I wish I could…"

"I know." He gave her a lopsided smile. "Me, too."

BECCA DIDN'T NEED a town poll or a recap in the local paper to gauge how she did in the debate; she had Olive Truitt in the front row. The more fiercely the tiny woman glared at her, the better Becca knew she was doing.

When Becca had first declared her intention to run, the mayor's wife had been all sweetness and light to her—saying that it was great to have a woman in the race, claiming that she admired Becca's gumption. But as it became clear that Becca had a real chance—thus jeopardizing Olive's standing as First Lady of Cupid's Bow—the woman's demeanor had changed. She and her two friends, Helen and Sissy, gossiped about Becca whenever they thought they could get away with it, not getting caught in outright lies, but certainly distorting the truth beyond recognition. Sierra had privately nicknamed Helen and Sissy "Hateful and Spiteful."

Sierra was also in the front row and her discreet thumbs-up signs throughout also let Becca know that she was doing well.

When Becca had arrived at the town hall two hours ago, Olive had cornered her by the water cooler. "I understand you hosted a poker game at your house. Very hospitable." Then she'd paused, a calculating gleam in her silver-gray eyes. "Although…one wonders if gambling is setting a good example for your son. Wouldn't want him to grow up with the same reckless disregard for money as his father."

Becca had been too furious to respond; the only

words that had leaped to mind would make her look
crass or volatile, and she refused to hand Olive that
ammunition. So she'd clenched her jaw and saved her
replies for the debate itself. Now, listening to Mayor
Truitt give his closing remarks before she took her turn,
she supposed she was lucky *he* hadn't brought up the
Johnston history with money, trying to smear her by
association to Colin. She figured the only reason he
hadn't was because he and Colin had done a number
of business deals together, deals that Truitt had made
substantial money on. The good mayor probably didn't
want to remind voters of his own association with the
shady real estate broker.

The debate had barely concluded when Becca's
phone buzzed with a text—from Sierra. YOU WERE
AWESOME! Apparently her friend thought it would be
undignified to tackle hug Becca and squeal her congratulations where other people could overhear, but
the string of emojis that popped up on Becca's phone
made Sierra's feelings clear.

Becca spent a few minutes shaking hands and thanking supporters, but the debate had been the draining
conclusion to an already long day. She couldn't wait to
get home. On the drive to her house, she felt a twinge
of regret that Sawyer hadn't been there tonight. He'd
volunteered to stay with Marc, and it wasn't as if he had
any stake in local politics, anyway. Still, she could just
imagine the expression on his face if he'd been there,
the pride shining in his hazel eyes. The unspoken but
unmistakable *way to go, sweetheart.*

Becca had wonderful friends—and greatly appreciated their support—but encouragement from Sawyer
lifted her in a way that was different than when Sierra

or Hadley verbally high-fived her. He liked to tease her about global domination, but sometimes the way he smiled at her did make her feel empowered enough to take over the world. *Becca Johnston, benevolent tyrant.*

She pulled into her driveway with a faint smile, ready for pajamas and pie and a stolen kiss or two.

The porch light wasn't on—despite the timer that was supposed to ensure she never had to climb the steps in the dark—and her eye was automatically drawn to the only light shining from the house, the bathroom window in the attic. Sawyer hadn't bothered to lower the blinds, and she could see just enough to know that he was shirtless and kneeling, partially out of view. Curious to find out what he was doing, she went inside. The downstairs was completely quiet; up above, she heard a shriek of laughter from Marc and the answering rumble of Sawyer's low voice. A high-pitched bark followed.

By the time Becca got to the top of the spiral staircase, she could also hear splashing sounds. The door to the attic apartment stood wide open and she went in to find Sawyer and her son giving Trouble a bath. From what Becca could tell, there was as much water on the floor as in the tub and the two guys were almost as wet as the puppy. Laughter burbled up inside her, and Sawyer whipped his head around, his expression guilty.

"You're home already!" He didn't sound particularly happy about that. "How'd it go?"

Hearing Becca's voice, Trouble lunged suddenly, trying to make a break from the tub. Water surged over the side as Sawyer tried to calm the puppy.

He glanced from the puddles on the tile back to Becca. "I, uh… You know I'll clean all this up, right?"

"Clean does seem to be the goal here," she said, biting back another laugh when the dog gave a full body shake, spraying Sawyer and Marc with droplets.

"Trouble rolled on somethin' dead," Marc announced, with a little boy's fascination for the gross. "She smelled worse than a skunk. Now she'll smell like shampoo."

"A definite improvement," Becca agreed. "You, however, are going to smell like wet dog. You'd better scoot down for a quick shower before bed."

His face fell. "Aww. But we aren't done!"

"I'll finish up," Sawyer said. "You listen to your mama. Okay?"

Marc nodded. "Yes, sir. Good night."

"Night, buddy." Sawyer gave her son a smile full of so much affection that tears pricked her eyes.

Years ago, Becca had thought she was on the path to a fairy-tale ending and had instead stumbled into divorce and scandal. She'd told herself that she was too wise now to make the same mistake again. But the sexiest man she knew was giving her dog a bath and looking at her kid with love. It created the illusion of family. Of happily-ever-after.

She followed her son downstairs, trying to keep her tears in check. There was no ever-after with a man like Sawyer. He'd walked away from his own family and didn't seem interested in putting down roots anywhere.

As a grown-up, she didn't think the most fantastical thing about fairy tales were the enchanted slippers or magic wands; it was that the charming princes were so ready and willing to commit. In real life, they all too often had one foot out the door.

BECCA'S BIG FESTIVAL challenge Wednesday afternoon was relocating three dozen fourth graders. They'd been scheduled to sing after the community theater performed a historic reenactment, but Becca deemed the ancient risers the kids stood on unsafe. The elementary school music teacher had twice requested that the collapsible stage be replaced, because the supports were starting to give way. So far, she'd been denied due to budgetary reasons, but after hearing how the metal creaked as the kids filed into place, Becca was already planning a fund-raiser to get new risers.

Meanwhile, she moved a cooking demonstration out of the gazebo to give the kids a place to perform, then headed off to find ice water and a portable fan for Marianne Schubert, who was having hot flashes in the arts and crafts tent. Once that was accomplished, she joined Lyndsay Whittmeyer and the boys, who were watching a glassblowing demonstration. Sawyer would be swinging by to pick up Marc and take him to his riding lesson.

"Hey." Lyndsay greeted her with a smile. "Got everything running to perfection?"

"Perfection? No. But I like to think I've brought order to the chaos."

"Your specialty. Honestly, you should give a seminar at the community center sometime on staying organized. I don't know how you do it…but you'll certainly be a darn good mayor."

"Fingers crossed."

"Sorry I couldn't make the debate the other night.

I was feeling under the weather, afraid I was coming down with something. Whatever it was, I'm glad it passed quickly."

"Staying home was the right call," Becca assured her. "You wouldn't want to risk getting everyone sick."

"I know. But I would've liked to watch you wipe the floor with Truitt—Sierra said it was awesome. Besides, there was something I wanted to ask you about. In person."

Becca raised an eyebrow. "Well, we're talking face-to-face now."

Casting a quick glance toward the boys, Lyndsay sidled a few feet away, then a few more. Once they'd put some distance between them and the kids, she asked, "So…you and the cowboy?"

Becca stalled. "What do you mean?"

"Is there something going on between the two of you? You looked pretty cuddly at the concert." She hesitated before adding, "You looked *happy*. And maybe it's none of my business, but you should know, I overheard the boys talking about it and—"

"The boys?" Her blood ran cold. Had Marc been talking about her and Sawyer as a couple? *Can you blame him? Sawyer's spent more quality time with him in the past two weeks than his father has in the past five years.* This was exactly the kind of disappointment she'd wanted to avoid for her son. "They don't think we're involved, do they?"

"I'm not sure. They clammed up when they noticed me. I just heard something about you and Sawyer and dancing. But, really, would it be such a bad thing to be involved with someone like him? You must have at least thought about it."

The urge to confide in her friend was overwhelming. Each day that brought them closer to goodbye threatened to crack Becca's calm, organized facade, leaving her in near-constant emotional turmoil. But as she debated whether to trust Lyndsay with her secret, she noticed Sissy Woytek in her peripheral vision. Best friend to the mayor's wife, Sissy was trying to look as though she wasn't shamelessly eavesdropping. Becca knew better than to care about what others thought of her personal life, yet she couldn't help feeling defensive, not just as a mayoral candidate but as a single mom. She didn't want others judging her affair and she sure as hell didn't want local gossip affecting Marc.

Instead of giving Lyndsay a straight answer—or worse, lying—she replied with a question of her own, one that wouldn't fuel any rumors from Sissy. "Does Sawyer really seem like the kind of guy I'd let myself fall for?"

Her friend was quiet for a long moment. "I guess not. He's certainly not anything like Colin. But you… Oh!" Her face flushed, and she raised her hand in a quick wave. "Hey, Sawyer."

Becca turned to find him behind her, gorgeous in the afternoon sunlight. "Everything go okay with the horses?" While some of the people going on the trail ride had horses of their own, some tourists would be on borrowed mounts provided by Brody and other local ranchers. Sawyer had gone with his friend to double-check the temperament and health of the animals before embarking on the three-day trip.

He nodded. "We're in good shape for the ride. Marc ready to go to his lesson?"

She signaled to her son, who trotted over with a

broad smile. Becca hugged him. "Have fun riding. I'll see you back home for dinner."

She watched the two of them walk up the hill together, Sawyer laughing at something the boy said while Marc gazed up with blatant hero worship. No, Sawyer was nothing like the slick, urbane, all-style-and-no-substance Colin. That was the problem. If he'd been more like her ex, she would have done a much better job of protecting her heart.

Does Sawyer really seem like the kind of guy I'd let myself fall for? The question echoed in Sawyer's head over and over until he found himself gnashing his teeth. Luckily, Marc and his instructor were on the other side of the ring, so the kid didn't notice Sawyer's mood. The boy had been excited for Sawyer to see him on horseback, so whenever Marc looked over, he did his best to look happy and encouraging.

But he hadn't felt very happy in the last forty-eight hours. He and Becca had shared an amazing night Sunday after the concert with no one the wiser about her midnight trip to visit a secret cowboy lover. It was beginning to chafe that she didn't want anyone to know about him. It felt…sordid.

Despite the incredibly intimate connection he'd felt with her Sunday night, he'd barely seen her Monday until she'd come home during Trouble's bath. Maybe it was just her busy schedule with the festival, but he had the damnedest sense that she'd been avoiding him since then. What had he done wrong?

Maybe the problem has nothing do with a what, a snide inner voice whispered, *but a who.* As in who he was—a rodeo cowboy with no college degree. Was she ashamed of him because he wasn't some businessman in a suit? Sawyer had left home feeling as if he wasn't good enough for his own family, so it didn't seem like a stretch that perhaps the future mayor of Cupid's Bow didn't think he was good enough for her, either.

She'd been dropping bizarre hints lately about career options. Write a book? Because that was a more prestigious, potentially more lucrative, job than bronc riding and ranch work? She'd said herself she'd been attracted to her ex because he was ambitious. *And how did that work out for you, sweetheart?*

It added to his cranky mood that Becca had been giving him little assignments, from asking him to drive Mrs. Spiegel to the mechanic's to putting him in charge of Marc's lesson today. Granted, Sawyer had told her he wanted to help, but the adorable novelty of her bossing him around was wearing off. His naturally rebellious nature was rising to the fore. Listening to her chide Molly bought back too many memories of Charlie lecturing him, and if Sawyer had to hear one more word about those lights on timers... What the hell was wrong with just turning lights on and off as needed? But no, Becca Johnston had to have things *her* way.

Yet beneath his increasing frustration was the suspicion that he might be overreacting. It was possible that his surliness had nothing to do with light timers and being cajoled into giving her son a ride. Maybe what really chapped Sawyer's ass was the knowledge that she was about to move on to a new important position, while he would be moving on with his life in an opposite direction. Would he see her again? *Hell, she barely lets you see her now*—at least, not in any way she was willing to admit in front of voters. It stung more than it should, and he was torn between wanting to get out of Cupid's Bow and away from the ache she caused, and wanting to stay as close to her for as long as he could.

BY THE TIME the guys returned from Marc's lesson, Becca had a spitting headache. She'd been arguing with Molly, who wanted to borrow the car to go hear a band in Turtle tomorrow. "Do you really think you've proved yourself responsible enough for that?" Becca had challenged, knowing her sister would be surrounded by men and booze in the club.

Molly had acted as if she had slapped her. Just as Becca was setting the table, her sister retreated to her room and refused to come out for dinner.

Although Sawyer didn't resort to stomping and slamming doors, his mood seemed almost as dark as Molly's. He didn't say much as he sat down.

"She's being impossible," Becca said, needing someone on her side.

He gave her a chiding glance over the top of the ice tea glass in his hand. "Maybe from her perspective, it seems like you're being impossible."

"Me? I'm the one doing her a favor!"

"And do you ever let her forget that? I know she's made mistakes, but that's how people learn. You can't be naive enough to think she's the first teenager to get dr—" Thankfully, he stopped himself, with a quick glance in Marc's direction. "People screw up. But constantly pointing it out can do more harm than good. Do you want to drive her away?"

"Is Aunt Molly going away?" Marc asked, sounding distraught.

Becca glared at Sawyer. "No, she's sticking around."

Unlike the cowboy. He had a lot of nerve, telling her how to manage her family when he didn't even speak to his own. She changed the subject for her son's sake. "How was your riding lesson?"

"Great." Marc's face brightened as he told her all about the horse and how much better he was getting and how he might be ready to try a canter or gallop.

She gave him a fond smile. "You're really enjoying it, aren't you?"

"A lot more than soccer," Sawyer muttered.

Both Becca and her son whipped their heads in his direction. Marc looked stricken. "Mr. Sawyer!"

"It's okay," Sawyer encouraged. "She should know."

"But…" His lip quivered.

Becca was livid. This was the second time in one meal Sawyer had offered his unsolicited opinion, and now he'd made her son uncomfortable. She glanced at Marc's mostly empty plate. "Would you like to be excused?"

He didn't have to be asked twice. Nodding, he scampered away from the table. Becca pressed her lips tightly together, trying not to explode while he was still in earshot.

Sawyer stood. "I think I'll go, too. I don't really have much of an appetite."

"Wait!" They needed to talk about this.

But the look he gave her made her suddenly question the wisdom of having the discussion now.

"Word of advice?" he said in a low voice. "When they elect you mayor, try not to order everyone around. They might stage a coup."

"You sound as melodramatic as Molly. Asking people to pitch in and giving people suggestions is not the same as 'ordering everyone around.' But while we're on the subject of ill-advised behavior? What was that about Marc and his soccer games?"

"He doesn't like it."

"I realize that."

Sawyer gave her a look of disgust. "But you make him play, anyway?"

She tried to silently count to ten to keep from shouting. "I don't 'make' him play. He wanted to sign up originally because Kenny Whittmeyer thought it would be cool, but didn't follow through. I've asked Marc point-blank if he likes playing. I'm trying to encourage him to be honest with me—if he could bring himself to say he wanted to quit, I'd pull him out. It's important to learn to stand up for yourself. Meanwhile, it's good exercise for him and he's getting better every week. Who knows? By next year, he might actually enjoy it." Sawyer wouldn't be here next year; he wouldn't even be here next month.

Angry that he'd become so enmeshed with their lives when he wasn't sticking around, she lashed out. "But none of this is *your* business. You're not his father. You're not even my boyfriend. You are—"

"Just a tenant. Got it." His expression was so cold that the temperature in the kitchen dropped ten degrees.

She hadn't meant to belittle him. She'd only been trying to establish boundaries, struggling after the fact to keep herself safely isolated. "Sawyer…"

"Nah, you're one hundred percent right, sweetheart." His bared his teeth in a sardonic smile. "As always."

WHEN SAWYER CAME downstairs in the morning after a brutally sleepless night, he found Becca at the table, bleary-eyed and cradling her head in her hands. Guilt twisted inside him; he hadn't meant to hurt her. But then, he hadn't been making the wisest decisions lately. He'd known from the start that an affair with a single mom would be complicated, much less a high-maintenance single mom who pushed all his buttons. Yet he'd ignored his own common sense.

"Sawyer." Her voice was raw, as if she had a cold. Or as if she'd been crying. "Glad I caught you before you headed out for the day."

"Actually…" He shifted his weight. "I'm headed out, period. I'm going to stay with Brody and Jazz tonight and leave with him for the trail ride tomorrow."

"What? I—"

"Truck's all loaded up," he said, trying to stick to his decision. If he remained here, there were only two likely outcomes—more fighting, which he didn't want. Or making up. Kissing each other, touching, growing closer…all of which would make their inevitable parting even worse. "I only came down here to leave this." He held up an envelope with his final rent payment and a note wishing her well.

"You were going to leave without saying goodbye?" She swallowed hard. "I guess taking off is what you do, though, huh?"

He stiffened at the accusation. "It wouldn't be permanent. I'll see you on the trail ride."

"Maybe not. I…have a lot to do before the election."

Liar. She was going to cancel because of him. The worst part was, he didn't know whether to be disappointed or relieved about not having to see her. Maybe it was best to get this whole thing over with. She obviously thought so if she was skipping the ride.

He tipped his hat toward her, his voice tight with emotion when he said, "Take care of yourself, Becca. And give Marc a hug for me."

"He's going to miss you."

I'll miss you both. But he wouldn't miss the way he'd felt the last few days—as if he was a dirty secret to be kept from voters. As if he was, yet again, not quite good enough. So he kept his words to himself and left, wincing when Trouble barked, as if she was calling him back. *Sorry, puppy.* It was time to go.

Chapter Thirteen

"You okay, sis?"

Becca glanced up from the book she hadn't been reading; she wasn't even sure what it was. "I've been better." The election was this week and she should be obsessing over her chances, trying to sway any last-minute undecided voters, but the days had been a hazy blur since Sawyer left. She knew her son was sad to see him go, but Marc's heartbreak was mitigated by school finally being out for the summer.

"I'm all ready for work," Molly said gently. "Still willing to drive me?"

Becca tossed the book on the coffee table, rising from the couch to get her keys. "Actually, why don't you take the car? I don't have anywhere I need to be today." She was taking a much-needed rest in the aftermath of what everyone was calling a very successful festival.

"Oh, wow, you're worse off than I thought." She hesitated. "You miss him, right?"

Becca blinked. Maybe her discreet affair hadn't been as discreet as she thought. "What do you mean?"

"He was gorgeous and great with Marc and even cooked sometimes. Plus, I saw how he looked at you. How could you *not* miss him?"

Excellent question—and one Becca was struggling to find the answer to. "Letting you use the car has nothing to do with any supposed feelings for Sawyer. I'm offering it because you're a smart adult working hard." In addition to the movie theater job, Molly was working minimal hours in the library, earning a stipend Hadley had managed to scrape together. "I've been thinking about it, and I need to treat you more like an adult. Maybe the reason I couldn't before was because I hated to admit we lost all those years. I was a crappy big sister to you."

"No you weren't!" Molly enveloped her in a tight hug. "You are the best."

"We'll see if you still feel that way in a minute," Becca said. "You should have adult responsibilities. I was thinking you could move into the attic apartment, come and go as you please—and that you should pay rent." Sawyer had accused her of constantly reminding Molly that this was a favor, that she was an imposition. Well, now that would change. "We can discuss the specifics tonight, but what do you think?"

Molly's eyes glittered. "I think I'm lucky to have you, and I won't let you down. I promise I'll drive exactly at the speed limit and come home right after my shift. Now, can I give you a piece of life advice?"

Becca raised her eyebrows, surprised, but trying to keep an open mind. "I suppose that's fair, after all the suggestions I've made."

"Go get your cowboy."

Loss burned in her chest, and Becca tried in vain not to picture his face. That teasing smile, those hazel eyes. "He's not mine. I don't even know where he is."

But Brody Davenport might. "All I need to make me happy are my family and winning this election."

Her chances had never seemed better. Recent informal polling after the festival put her way ahead of Truitt. She should be feeling confident and eager. Not hollow.

Molly eyed her with a combination of skepticism and pity. "You're sure that's all you need?"

"Well…and key lime pie." And time. She'd healed from her divorce over time. Wouldn't this be the same? In a few weeks, she'd be so busy running this town, she'd barely remember Sawyer McCall.

"I HOPE I'M not interrupting, but can I talk to you for a minute, Madam Mayor?"

Becca turned from the owner of the bowling alley, who'd been telling her how glad local business owners were that she'd won, to see Sierra Bailey, especially gorgeous in a strappy green cocktail dress. Plenty of wedding receptions had been held in the community center "ballroom," but tonight it had been elegantly decorated for Becca's victory party. She was thrilled, but feeling slightly overwhelmed by all the congratulations and people who wanted to shake her hand. It would be relaxing to just talk to a friend for a few moments.

She flashed Sierra a grateful smile. "You're allowed the occasional interruption—I couldn't have done this without you! If you'll excuse me for a moment?" she asked the bowling-alley manager.

"Absolutely. Guest of honor needs to circulate." He held up his glass. "I need a refill, anyway." With a polite nod to Sierra, he ambled toward the cash bar.

"I've been dying for a chance to get you alone all night!" Sierra said. "Short of stalking you on your way to use the ladies' room, this seemed like my best opportunity."

"It has been hectic. Good hectic, obviously. Who could possibly complain about such an outpouring of felicitations?" Odd, though, that she had talked to dozens of people tonight and still felt so lonely. "What can I do for you?"

Sierra bit her lip. "Okay, I hope this isn't an incredibly insensitive faux pas—I know tonight's a big night for you—but I have something I need to tell you."

"Out with it then." Of all Becca's friends, Sierra was the one who most bluntly spoke her mind. Now that she had her attention, what could be slowing her down? Unless she was afraid of ruining Becca's jubilant mood? "Is it bad news? Did Truitt demand a recount or something?"

"Nothing like that! Just the opposite. I have great news." She leaned close so that Becca could hear her whisper over the chatter of partygoers. "I'm engaged."

Becca barely managed to contain an undignified whoop of glee. "Seriously? Oh, honey, that's fantastic!" She squashed her friend in a hug that no doubt wrinkled both their dresses. "When did this happen?"

"This morning. He proposed on a napkin."

"He what?" Becca raised an eyebrow, about to be disappointed in Jarrett. He'd lived his whole life in Cupid's Bow and knew all the most romantic places. What was this nonsense about a napkin?

Sierra, however, was beaming, no trace of disappointment in her glowing expression. "It's this thing he does...leaves me romantic notes next to my morning coffee, written on napkins. This morning's said 'Will you marry me?' Then when I said yes, we ditched the coffee in favor of celebratory mimosas, and he carried me back to our bedroom and—" Her cheeks went rosy. "Well, it was all much more romantic than it probably sounds."

"Actually, it *does* sound romantic." The idea of waking up to someone who adored you each morning? Someone who showed his affection by making coffee and jotting love notes? A twinge went through Becca as she thought of the times she and Sawyer had shared in her kitchen, those predawn moments when it had been just the two of them, him teasing her over the rim of his coffee mug and making her grin even though smiling at 6:00 a.m. seemed vaguely unnatural.

Enough with the melancholy. Tonight is a celebration! Not just for her, but for one of her closest friends. "So is there a ring yet?" she asked, looking down at Sierra's hand.

"Yes, but I didn't wear it tonight. We didn't want to upstage you with a public announcement—only family knows—but I had to tell you! I'm hoping you'll be my maid of honor." Sierra grinned. "If you're not *too* busy running Cupid's Bow."

"Oh, I will be such a good maid of honor," Becca vowed, touched that Sierra had asked her. "I'm very detail oriented. And I have pull. Anything you two want for the ceremony, it's done."

"See? This is why you're my favorite control freak! But honestly—" she sighed, peering through the crowd until her gaze landed on her handsome rancher "—the main thing I want for the ceremony is just to walk down the aisle to that guy right there."

As if he sensed her gaze, Jarrett glanced up from the conversation he was having with Sierra's coworker Manuel. When his eyes locked with his fiancée's, his expression became so intimately tender that Becca almost felt like a voyeur standing there. The two of them were going to be so happy together—a fairy-tale ending she could believe in.

No, what they had was better than a fairy tale. It was a partnership.

That's what I want. And yet she was used to running her own household, unaccustomed to thinking of anyone as an equal partner. She knew from her divorce that it was a risk, depending on someone and suddenly waking up one day to find they were no longer there. But for happiness like Sierra and Jarrett shared, wasn't it worth the attempt?

SAWYER SMILED AT his family, touched to be here sharing Sunday dinner with them for the first time in years. When he'd come home five days ago, things had been awkward at first, tentative. It had probably helped smooth the way when Sawyer declined his brother's offer to formally become part owner in the ranch.

"I appreciate it," Sawyer had said sincerely. "But this isn't where I want to be permanently. I'm still weighing options."

"Oh, thank God." Charlie had looked relieved. "Because the offer was genuine, but I still have some control-freak tendencies."

Sawyer had clapped him on the back, his smile bittersweet. "Some of my favorite people do."

Since that conversation, tensions in the house had eased considerably. And now his mother was standing, her eyes glistening with emotion, honoring him with a toast. "To Sawyer. All I've wanted was for you to make peace with your brother and father, return to the bosom of your family. And my prayers have been answered!" Smiling, she pressed a hand to her heart. "Now, are you going to leave of your own volition, or do I have to kick you out?"

He blinked. "Pardon?"

"Honey, we love having you on the ranch, and you're always welcome," she said. "But, um, isn't there somewhere else you'd rather be?"

"She means with Becca," Charlie added, "in case you're too much of a chucklehead to suss that out for yourself."

"Wh-what?"

"Oh, come on." Charlie rolled his eyes. "You've been to how many places since we saw you last, won how many rodeos? But have you been telling us about any of them? No. We keep hearing stories about your landlady and a little town called Cupid's Bow."

Even taciturn Charles Sr. spoke up. "You're obviously in love with the girl, so she must be special. McCall men don't run from commitment." The loving glance he exchanged with his wife was mirrored at the other end of the table between Charlie and Gwen.

Sawyer should have felt uncomfortable, like a fifth wheel. Instead, what he experienced was a sharp mental clarity that had eluded him since he'd left Cupid's Bow with a bruised ego and a half-assed plan to make amends with his family. He *was* being a chucklehead. Did he want to stay here, seeing Becca only in the *Cupid's Bow Clarion* articles he looked up at 3:00 a.m. like some sort of internet stalker, or did he want to admit that he should have been more patient? More understanding about her reservations? She had a child to think about and a divorce behind her; she couldn't just throw herself headlong into a relationship with a guy she'd known less than a month. The only reason Sawyer had even wanted her to was because he'd fallen so hard for her.

He turned to his older brother. "You are absolutely right."

Charlie leaned back in his chair. "You want to run that by me again?"

Sawyer laughed. "No. Once-in-a-lifetime kind of thing."

"Still… Sawyer McCall willing to say I was right. I guess miracles do happen."

Good. Because he might need one to make things right with Becca.

SAYING GOODBYE TO his family hadn't been difficult, since Sawyer didn't plan to wait so long this time before seeing them again. Still, he appreciated the few minutes of privacy with Charlie out by his truck. He had a few things he needed to say to his brother.

But Charlie was staring past him, squinting at a minivan coming down the drive. "Now, who do you suppose that is?"

Sawyer's heart turned over in his chest, thudding in wild hope. "She's here."

"Becca?" Charlie grinned, then started loping toward the house. He called over his shoulder, "Try not to screw this up, man."

Sawyer took deep breaths, but the sight of her as she climbed out of the van shook his composure. God, he'd missed her. "B-Becca?" He couldn't believe he was seeing her in person.

Her smile was crooked, endearingly uncertain. "Surprised?"

"Stunned. What are you doing here? Not that I'm unhappy to see you," he hastily added.

"I needed to talk to you—about us. If there's still a chance we can be an 'us.' Sawyer, I'm so sorry about how I handled our relationship." Guilt shone in her eyes. "I want to be with you. I want everyone in Cupid's Bow to know, which probably doesn't mean as much to you now that the election's over—"

"Are you kidding me, woman?" He reached for her, tugging her into his arms. She wanted him. Enough to track him down and drive all the way here, down unpaved roads MapQuest didn't know existed, to tell him in person. "It means more than I can put into words. My life is flexible, ungrounded. I should have recognized that, with all your responsibilities, you have to be more cautious. I pushed too hard, and I'm sorry."

He crushed her in a fierce hug. Having spent the last couple miserable weeks without her, he never wanted to let her go again. He expelled a breath that was half groan, half chuckle. "Dammit, I was going to ride back into town and sweep you off your feet, but you beat me to it." That was his Becca; she knew her own mind and took action.

She met his eyes, her gaze searching. "You aren't really annoyed I'm here, are you?"

"Hell, no. I'm annoyed at myself for letting wounded pride come between us, but mostly I just feel grateful." He wanted to kiss her with all the pent-up need and longing he felt, but was intensely aware of the witnesses no doubt crowded together at his mother's kitchen window.

Instead, he rocked back on his heels and cupped Becca's face in his hands. "I love you."

"I love you, too."

Joy welled inside him—not just happiness, but a sense of contented, soul-deep belonging. "I was serious about being on my way to see you." He jerked his chin toward the bags that sat in his truck. "I'm willing to make Cupid's Bow my home…if you're okay with that."

"There's nothing I'd like more. I should warn you, though—the attic's taken. Molly just paid me rent for the whole month. Seems wrong to kick her out."

"I wouldn't expect to live with you." Not until everyone saw how serious they were and he could get Marc's blessing on proposing to his mama. "How would that look, the mayor of Cupid's Bow moving a boy toy in so soon after the election?"

She gave him a lopsided smile. "You assume I won?"

"I believed in you, yeah, but… I looked it up online just to make sure. Congratulations, Madam Mayor. I'm proud of you." To hell with the onlookers. He *had* to kiss her.

She eagerly met him halfway, rising up on her tiptoes and clutching at his shoulders. Their fervent kiss was a celebration, a reunion, a pledge. When he finally forced himself to pull away, they were both gasping for air.

"I desperately want to get you alone," he growled, "but my family will never forgive me if I don't introduce you first."

"I want to meet them, too." Yet she hesitated, her expression endearingly vulnerable. "They just got you back. Brody said you and your brother are getting along better than you have in a decade. Will they resent my taking you away from home?"

"Home is with you." Was it too soon to say something of that magnitude?

Apparently not. She beamed at him with so much love he felt invincible. He could win every rodeo in the world and not feel anything as sweet as the triumph of knowing he'd won her heart.

Lacing his fingers through hers, he led her toward the house. "I really do like Cupid's Bow, and I've put out some feelers for jobs in the area. But the important part is that we're together. I want to be where you are, want to help you with Marc—not that you need it," he said, backpedaling.

She squeezed his hand. "Sure I do. Everyone can use *some* help, and there's no one I'd rather turn to. I need your perspective and your ability to make me laugh when I least expect it. And the way you can block out the rest of the world with your kiss," she added huskily.

He stopped, trying to recall why they had to go inside instead of ducking into the barn and frantically undressing each other.

Her cheeks grew rosy under his stare, and she attempted a breezy tone. "Plus, there's the obvious—I need you to keep me too busy to accidentally attempt global domination."

"Oh, I have some ideas about how we could occupy your time." He raised her hand to his lips, brushing a quick kiss across her knuckles. "But, sweetheart? If you ever want to take over the world, I'll be right there beside you, cheering you on." And feeling damn lucky that she'd altered *his* world, now and forever.

* * * * *

If you loved this novel, don't miss the next book in Tanya Michaels's CUPID'S BOW, TEXAS *series, coming in 2018 from Harlequin Western Romance!*

And check out previous books in the series:
FALLING FOR THE SHERIFF
FALLING FOR THE RANCHER
THE CHRISTMAS TRIPLETS

Get 2 Free Books,

◆HARLEQUIN® Western Romance

Plus 2 Free Gifts—
just for trying the
Reader Service!

HWRI7R

SPECIAL EXCERPT FROM

◆ **HARLEQUIN**®
™

Western Romance

*Sage Lockhart and Nick Monroe are friends with
benefits. When Sage asks Nick to make her dream of
having a family come true, he agrees...only because he
is secretly in love with her!*

*Read on for a sneak preview of
WANTED: TEXAS DADDY,
the latest book in Cathy Gillen Thacker's series
TEXAS LEGACIES: THE LOCKHARTS.*

"You want to have my baby," Nick Monroe repeated
slowly, leading the two saddled horses out of the stables.

Sage Lockhart slid a booted foot into the stirrup and
swung herself up. She'd figured the Monroe Ranch was
the perfect place to have this discussion. Not only was it
Nick's ancestral home, but with Nick the only one living
there now, it was completely private.

She drew her flat-brimmed hat straight across her
brow. "An unexpected request, I know."

Yet, she realized as she studied him, noting that the
color of his eyes was the same deep blue as the big Texas
sky above, he didn't look all that shocked.

For he better than anyone knew how much she wanted a
child. They'd grown quite close ever since she'd returned
to Texas, to claim her inheritance from her late father and
help her mother weather a scandal that had rocked the
Lockhart family to the core.

She drew a deep, bolstering breath. "The idea of a complete stranger fathering my child is becoming increasingly unappealing." When they reached their favorite picnic spot, she swung herself out of the saddle and watched as Nick tied their horses to a tree.

Nick grinned, as if pleased to hear she was a one-man woman, at least in this respect.

He looked at her from beneath the brim of his hat. "Which is why you're asking me?" he countered in the rough, sexy tone she'd fallen in love with the first second she had heard it. "Because you know me?"

Sage locked eyes with him, not sure whether he was teasing her or not. One thing she knew for sure: there hadn't been a time since they'd first met that she *hadn't* wanted him.

"Or because," he continued flirtatiously, as he unscrewed the lid on his thermos, "you have a hankering for my DNA?"

Aware the only appetite she had now was not for food, she quipped, "How about both?"

Don't miss WANTED: TEXAS DADDY
by Cathy Gillen Thacker, available June 2017 wherever
Harlequin® Western Romance
books and ebooks are sold.

www.Harlequin.com

HWREXP0517